MOMENTS
OF
MALEVOLENCE

Dedication

"Sit there and take it like a good girl."
You, dirty, dirty girl, I was talking about the book...

Alaska

I lie to one of the city's most ruthless men.
And it feels so good.
Deception is a drug, and I'm quickly becoming an addict.
Each time we speak, Zuko has no idea it's me.
The lie tastes sweet leaving my mouth.
I couldn't stop now, even if I wanted to—which I don't.
He thinks our conversations are more than just sex.
He's wrong.
The intimacy he feels is all a facade.
Until the day an embodiment of my darkest fantasies walks into my bar, and his unmistakable voice sends a shiver down my spine.
It turns out I'm *not* the one in control.
But when he calls tonight, and he will, I'll be ready…
… with a lie.

Zuko

My job is to hunt. Dispose of problems like they never existed. And I'm incredibly good at my job.

It's brutal and violent. But, then again, so I am.

I crave destruction. Death is merely a consequence of my dark pursuits.

And I won't lose a wink of sleep over it, either.

Nothing bothers me.

No one affects me.

Except the vixen with the lilac hair.

When I reveal my true self to her, she laughs it off, enticed by the game we play.

She's keeping secrets.

And I know *all* about prying information out of people.

She won't like my methods.

But I'll keep playing her little game until I decide what to do about her.

I can't tell if she is destined to be my wife…

… or my next victim.

ONE

Zuko

"YOU'VE REACHED Sage from You Beat It, We Spit It. First, let's start with your name…"

That incredible voice rings through my phone, and I sit up a little straighter at the sound.

A swan. For some reason, her voice reminds me of a swan, lord fucking knows why, it's not like they talk… But I bet if it did, it would sound like her—all grace and elegance with a melodic glide that can make a grown man moan.

"Hello?" There she goes again, making my cock hard with that damn voice.

Fuck.

Fuck.

"Sage…" She pauses at my voice, and I hear

her breathing pick up. "You've been working a lot lately," I tell her.

"That just proves you've been calling a lot lately," she replies back.

Little does she know just how many times I call —many more than she can imagine. Hearing her voice eases a lot of shit stirring inside me and I fucking hate it, because no one should hold that much power without knowing it.

I can't remember the first time I called or how I got the number. But now I treat it like a druggie treats crack, and I'm fucking milking it for all it's worth.

That voice.

The way she says my name.

"Are you still there, Zuko?" She doesn't say it in a voice of concern, more like boredom and one that implies I need to hurry up so she can get back to whatever it is she was doing.

Women either drop to their knees for me or run. *Her?* Well, she doesn't seem to care.

And I like that about her.

A lot.

I hear her chewing gum on the other end of the line and listen as she blows a bubble and it pops loudly into the receiver.

"Yes," I answer.

"Good. So how do you want to do this tonight?" she asks. "Would you like me to start by telling you how wet I am at hearing your sinful-as-fuck voice echo through the phone and calling my name? You know I enjoy it when you call my name," she purrs.

"It's not your real name, now, is it?" I reply. "Tell me your real name," I urge.

She laughs. It's not a playful noise, more of a "yeah, fucking right, not happening" sound.

"Zuko. Is that even your *real name*? It sounds made up." A change of subject—she is so very good at deflecting.

"Yes, it is my name. Why would I give you a fake name?"

"Okay, we can agree to disagree, *Zuko*." She says my name long and drawn out as it rolls off her tongue. "How would you like today to go?"

"Tell me… What did you do today?" I ask.

"Is that what you really want to hear?"

"Yes."

"Okay. First, you tell me what you did."

"I sliced a man's throat because he annoyed me. It was bloody."

"You always say the weirdest shit." I can

3

imagine her head shaking and the look on her face —pure boredom.

"What color is your hair?" I ask.

"Blue," she says without missing a beat. "Though, I may change it tomorrow."

"Why blue?"

"Because I was depressed this week and decided my hair should match my mood." My lips pull at the side of my mouth. "Would blue hair bother you?" she asks.

"No. Now tell me your name."

"It's Sage. We've had this discussion. Honestly, this topic is getting boring, and you're wasting my time. I'm working here, Zuko, so let's do what you're paying me to do, or shall we move on."

"You don't want to talk to me anymore?" I ask.

"If it's dirty."

"Go on… Tell me about your tits," I urge.

I'm not sure when it changed, where I became more obsessed with listening to her than the actual words she speaks to me. But it's addicting, tempting, and incredibly arousing.

"Hmm… You want to know how my fingers are sliding in my bra right now to touch my pink, taut nipples?" she whispers. "Or how wet the thought of you makes me?"

I say nothing—she's used to it.

She continues. "Zuko, right now I'm imagining your hands gripping me, so fucking roughly it's going to leave bruises... Marks wherever you touch me. Your hands are big, I know they are. And I'll be marked by you for all to see. You'd like that, wouldn't you? Your hands marking me, sliding over my ass, slapping it hard. Hmm..." She gives me her best moan, and I wonder if her real ones sound the same.

Probably different.

Definitely different.

"I'm going to find you, Sage, and when I do—"

She hangs up every time.

This time is no different.

Fucking burner phone.

TWO

Alaska

I FUCKING HATE MY JOB.

Despise it.

But it pays well.

And idiots are willing to pay.

Except Zuko.

He pays well, and is far from an idiot, I think.

That can't be his real name, but I have a feeling he hasn't got a reason to lie. His voice is so deep that whenever he does call me, I wonder why he needs my services. A voice like his should be making women drop to their knees to look up at him through their lashes with want and need.

He must be fucked-up.

Something has to be wrong with him.

I mean, apart from the fucked-up shit he always tells me.

Who says that kind of stuff so casually?

I killed a man…

What the fuck does that mean!

I have another job working at a bar dressed as a cowgirl, complete with boots, a pair of shorts that ride up my ass, and mini shirts.

That job I don't hate quite as much. The tips are good, but the pay is way better at my telephone sex job.

It's how I'm able to afford my condo.

We didn't have money when I was growing up. So now that I have it, you bet your ass I'm spending it on shit I like which includes living lavishly. I have no man to pay for luxuries, so I work two jobs and have for years. And it works for me.

"Alaska." My boss grinds his jaw when he sees me. "You knew tonight was pink."

I glance at my black boots in my hand, black shirt, and booty shorts and smirk at him. "You know I don't own anything pink. Why would you even suggest such a thing?" I give him an eye roll and stroll past him.

"If you didn't have VIPs who come only to see you, you know I'd fire you, right?" he yells out after me as I walk off. I give him a wave but say nothing in return.

I'm sexy. It's something I own. I paid a lot for my tits and workout regularly to keep my body in shape. I am proud of it. I know I can't do these types of jobs forever. Well, not this type of waitressing, but the other I can. So I milk it, and why the fuck not? Men have milked women for their appearance since the beginning of time, and now it's time we took back our power without the judgment that comes along with it and milk that shit ourselves.

So I sell my voice for sex over the phone.

Let men ogle my body for great tips that put a marvelous roof over my head.

What's the fucking issue with that? Nothing.

"Alaska, gosh. Thank fuck you're here." Louise puts me in one of her awkward hugs. I swear she does it knowing how much I hate them.

Hugging is awkward, and nobody can tell me any different. For the most part you are getting someone else's boobs or crotch pretty damn close to your own. You then have to contend with said person's perfume or cologne or God forbid body odor. And I'm not even going to talk about breath. So yeah, awkward.

I shrug her off, but she isn't offended. She never is.

"We have super-duper VIPs tonight. And I know you have your regulars who book you well in advance every weekend, but do you think you can help your best friend out?" She pouts, her bottom lip sticking out.

"Who said you are my best friend?" I ask, brow raised.

To be honest, she's probably my only friend. Louise is loud and speaks to everyone, but she talks to me the most. Only fucking God knows why.

She waves me off. Not only does she not care about my hug brush offs, but she's also never offended by my rude comments either.

Why? Again, I have no idea.

I guess it's one of the reasons I like her; she doesn't get offended by what I say, where the other girls here call me a bitch.

I am, and I don't give two fucks about what they think.

I have no qualms with the other girls hating me or talking behind my back.

I'm here to make money, not fucking friends.

"What do you need help with?" I ask, opening my locker and putting my things inside.

When she doesn't answer right away, I turn to look at her. "Louise, spit it out."

"Jeff told me not to ask for help."

"That ship sailed, didn't it? Besides when do I ever listen to Jeff?" I smirk. "Now, tell me, what do you need help with?"

"Well, I know the men coming in tonight. They're from where I grew up. They are…"

"What?" I ask when she trails off.

"Scary. And they terrify me."

"You can't have my area, Louise. You know you can't. My regulars don't want you."

"I know. They want you. But I was hoping I could help you, make it easier for you to help me." She bites her lip.

"Louise, you know how to make people warm up to you. Are you sure you can't do this one yourself?"

She starts shaking her head, slowly at first, and then picks up the pace the more the panic rises in her eyes. "No, please don't make me." Her eyes are wide, and then I notice a visible shudder run down her body. Louise never shows fear. She's always bubbly. Always.

"Okay, I'll help. I'll take their orders, and you

deliver. That's the best I can offer. I have my own tables I need to manage."

She leans in and throws her arms around my neck, and yells in my ear, "I love you. So, so much," before she pulls away. My hands stay at my sides. "You don't know what this means to me. These men…" Her whole body shakes and she bites her lip.

"I'm sure they aren't *that* bad."

"They never come to places like this. Bars aren't what they do."

"Bars are what everyone does," I remind her.

She chews her bottom lip nervously. "No, not these men. When I saw their names, I didn't believe they could possibly come here. But if it is really them…" She sucks in a breath. "They have a reputation, and its known. These are three men you never want on your bad side."

"Well, maybe someone is just using their names, and you might get off easy." I smile knowing how far-fetched it sounds but trying to make her feel better anyway.

"If someone is, then they have a death wish," she murmurs under her breath before she turns and walks away. I shake my head, having never seen

Louise this worked up over anything. She is always bubbly and doesn't let anything get to her.

Kicking off my slides, I pull on my black cowboy boots. When I glance up, Sarah's standing there applying her pink lipstick and staring at me.

"It's meant to be pink tonight. Do you ever fucking listen?"

I hate Sarah as much as she hates me.

Ignoring her, I throw my slides into my locker and turn my back on her before I start to wander out.

"I can't wait for the day they fire you," she says loud enough for me to hear.

"Sarah, have you ever seen blackness before?" I ask, and she scrunches up her nose at my question.

"Who even says shit like that? Blackness? Do you even speak English?"

"Blackness is what happens when I slam your head into this locker so hard that all you see is black. So shut your fucking mouth before I do just that."

She whips her inky hair over her shoulder and turns before storming off.

Maybe I should have slammed her fucking head anyway.

But I have to remind myself—no violence, I'm a

new person now. I don't have to slam heads into lockers because someone has pissed me off.

No, I'm not that person anymore.

But I could be if Sarah fucking pisses me off *one more time*.

———

Louise pulls me by my arm to her area.

My guys are all taken care of for now, and luckily for her, her men were late. So it all worked out well in the end.

"They recognize me," she whispers.

"They do?" I ask, rolling my eyes.

"Yes, I went to school with the twins. They don't talk much." Her grip tightens on my arm as she continues pulling me along.

"You really can't do the rest yourself? You've already served them, and it is your job," I state.

"They didn't want to order, so I stepped away and got you. See if you can get them to order."

Technically, they don't have to order anything. They pay a large fee for the private tables as it is, but it's all about up-sell, up-sell, up-sell. The more we up-sell the larger the tips.

When we get to the edge of where they are

seated Louise stops and turns to me. "I'll go and see if your men want any more drinks while you look after *them*." She says "them" as if they are forbidden. When I don't move, she pinches her lips together. "Please," she begs.

"You owe me so big, you know that, right?" I say, pushing my lilac hair behind my ear. I should have dyed it pink. That would have made the boss happy, too bad I am not about making anyone happy but myself.

Louise leans up and kisses my cheek before she runs off, leaving me standing there. I sigh and step around the corner where I am immediately met with three sets of eyes. They're all staring at me as I climb the stairs until I'm standing directly in front of them. I don't know the color of their eyes, but their stares are laden with darkness, and I feel them creeping all over my body.

"Howdy, boys." I smile as I voice the line we have to say when greeting customers. Cowboy bar, remember? And we aren't even in Texas. Good Lord. "I know Louise has served you already." I check and notice all the alcohol is untouched. *Weird.* "But I was hoping I could persuade you to partake in some of our top-shelf liquor." When none of them respond, I open my mouth to go for a different angle when someone else walks up the stairs. This guy offers me a smile as he takes a seat.

"Bring us the Macallan," he says.

"The thirty year old?" I ask.

"Yes."

"We only serve that by the bottle."

"Yes, yes." He waves me off. He turns to the three other men. "We're celebrating." I start to move when another voice stops me, sending shivers all over my body.

"What's your name?"

That voice—it's familiar.

No, it can't be. Surely not. Goosebumps dot my skin as my brain matches up the name with my most regular customer. I spin around to find the speaker and come face to face with a man who is so deadly gorgeous I immediately know he isn't *my* Zuko. I don't see anyone who would call to have sex over the phone; this man needs no help in that department based on his looks alone.

"My name's Alaska. Holla if you need anything." I give him a wink and step away.

As soon as I get to the bar to give my order, Louise is back and gluing herself to me.

"Did they ask where I went?" she whispers.

"No, they hardly spoke. Some new guy came in

and ordered for them." She checks over her shoulder and sucks in a breath.

"That's Grayson. He's younger, but as far as I know, he is the only friend they have," she shrugs. "Well he's the only one they are seen speaking to at least. He also owns the sex club downtown." I've heard of that place, even considered getting a job there before I found the phone sex job. Plus, I find hugs weird, so letting someone touch me, especially for money, would be way worse. Just thinking about it gives me the shivers.

No, thank you.

"So they can afford the alcohol they just ordered?" I ask her.

She nods her head. "Absolutely. They could probably buy this place if they wanted to." She laughs. "You wouldn't think it, considering we come from the same beat-down, fucked-up area…" She pauses. "We made our way out of it, though I hear they still live there. Lord knows why."

I grab the drinks and prepare to deliver them when she speaks again. "They are devils, Alaska, remember that." I smile at her words; trouble, we all love a little bit of it.

THREE

Zuko

I'M NOT one to pick up chicks from bars, but this one has piqued my interest. What is it about her?

It can't be that fake smile she gives each of us, as if we think she's happy to be here and serving us.

No. It has to be something else.

But what?

"Why are you looking at her like that?" Kyson nudges me, but I don't bother turning to him.

"Do you want her to stay?" Grayson asks.

I glance his way, and he's raising a brow, waiting for me to answer him. I say nothing and sit back as I watch her step up the stairs and then pour the whiskey into the glasses. She hands Grayson his and once again smiles that well-rehearsed fake smile she has mastered so well. Then she does the same to my brothers before she gets to me. When she offers me the drink, my gaze moves from the glass to her. My hands are in my lap, and I make no move to grab the glass. She glances down at my hands, then at me before she stands to her full height.

"No drink?" she asks, smiling. "Anything else I can get you if you don't want whiskey?"

I bite the inside of my lip as I watch her. Most women would be uncomfortable with my stare, but she gives it straight back with no hesitation whatsoever.

What is it about her?

She waits for a few beats before she places the glass on the tray and turns her attention to the other guys. "Anything else I can get you all?"

"No, that will be all for now," Grayson states. She nods and goes to leave, but she takes one last glance at me, and I see the villain in her eyes, the one who wants to come out to play. She pins me with a stare as if to say, "fuck you," then grins before she saunters off.

"You could talk to her, you know," Grayson mutters.

My brothers and I don't socialize. Frankly, we fucking hate everyone. Even my own brothers get on my very last nerve. Grayson was a little punk on our street that somehow, we let in our inner circle, which is something we don't usually do. And we haven't been able to get rid of him since.

He's like glue, he just sticks.

But he's loyal.

I raise an impatient brow at Grayson words, but he just shakes his head before he turns and starts talking to the twins.

Growing up we didn't know what we wanted to do with our lives. We figured the only way to make money was drugs—either buying or selling. We did that for a bit until I witnessed a murder.

Right in front of my eyes.

He was an older man and wore a black ski mask and all-black clothing.

I wanted to laugh at the irony of it.

It was straight out of the damn movies.

He killed our neighbor and climbed out the window before he lit a cigarette, took off his mask, and set the house on fire. He spotted me, smirked, and walked over, his hand running through his hair.

"Trying to work out… Should I kill you where you stand, kid," he'd said, as the house behind him went up like a kindling box, and he paid no attention to it. "But I see that gleam in your eyes." He leaned in close, slipped me a phone, and whispered,

"Do you want to do something dangerous for the rest of your life?"

I pulled back and stared at him.

How did he know?

He didn't even wait for me to answer as he nodded his head. "Answer when I call." He walked off, and I never looked back. When he called my phone two days later, I answered. When he said to meet him, I listened. And when I rolled up to the arranged meeting spot, there were five other teenagers there as well. I was the youngest, but that didn't mean shit.

We were being trained by special operations soldiers, the ones who loved killing so much that when they pulled out of service, they started to do their own dirty shit.

It was the most painful thing I had ever done in my life.

The training was intense, and it took a good year before I was allowed my first kill.

I fucked it up, but Pops—that's what the man who gave me the phone liked to be called—fixed it.

I never fucked up a kill after that.

A year later, Pops asked about my brothers. He was creating his own army and I was his special soldier.

He figured because he could mold me, my brothers would be great assets as well.

And he was right.

They were.

The three of us became his secret weapons. He stopped training other people after that. The men he had trained before my brothers and me, and even those after, he let go, or possibly killed, I don't know and don't care to ask.

Pops was lethal, but I had become even more lethal with time.

And in turn, my brothers did as well.

We were deadly.

Destructive.

Evil.

To this day, we still work for Pops. But he isn't the only place we get jobs now.

Killing is what we are good at.

Killing is our business.

Why would we limit ourselves to one person who gives us work when we have the whole fucking world at our fingertips?

FOUR

Alaska

TALK ABOUT INTIMIDATING.

All those men are daunting.

But that one that looks like he walked straight in from an all-black party, with eyes as green as the forest and lips curved into the perfect heart shape, is the most haunting of them all.

A little too intense for me.

"They're asking for you," Louise says as I attempt to deliver drinks to my original tables. She goes to take them from me, but I shake my head.

"I need the tips, Louise. Why the fuck do you think I work here? Those men haven't tipped me anything. My table…" I nod to where my customers are seated, "tip every time I bring them drinks."

She bites her lip. "Okay, sorry. I'll tell them

you're busy." She turns away, and a small part of me feels bad, but I shake it off and march straight past the area with the intense, powerful men, and I don't spare them a glance as I head to my tables.

My customers grin at me, and one even slaps my ass—fucking bastard. I can't help the cringe and want to break his hand, but instead, I smile like a good girl because I know he will tip me well. I turn, handing him his drink, and he tips me a hundred-dollar bill and leans up so his smelly breath is next to my ear as he speaks.

"Come on, darlin', come home with me. I can show you how to ride a cowboy. We can even leave those boots on."

Talk about ew.

His belly is hanging over his pants, his hair is half missing, his teeth need a good brush with an angle grinder, and he stinks.

The rest, I can deal with.

I've fucked a cuddly teddy bear before, and he was the best man to ever give me head. *The. Best.*

But someone who stinks and has bad breath? That's a hard no.

I wouldn't say I'm all that picky.

But I do have standards, and I know what I want.

I don't want commitment.

I want a man who will throw me against the wall and fuck me good and hard.

This man cannot do that.

Of that, I am sure.

"I'm good, but thanks anyway." I give my best smile as I turn to leave. He reaches for me again, and I manage to sidestep him as I shift away from their booth. Just as I reach the bottom of the steps with tray in hand, I slam into a hard body. When I peek up, the man from Louise's table who asked my name is standing before me. He reaches out and steadies me, his hand gripping my waist, so I don't fall. As soon as I'm stable, his hand drops away from my body like it felt wrong to touch me.

It didn't.

Not for me anyway.

"Sorry, didn't see you there." I smile at him. He stares past me and says nothing, then his jaw locks in a hard glare before those green eyes find mine. Seeing him this close with only a tray between us, I notice the flecks of gold in his eyes.

Those eyes—they stare straight through you.

Deadly.

If I were a smart woman, I would look away.

But I live on the edge, and he seems like a man

it would be fun to annoy, and despite all the warnings I have received I just can't help myself with him.

I go to wonder why, but instantly ignore that feeling and smile up at him.

"Do you plan to just stand there, or do you intend to move?" I ask as he continues staring at me.

He doesn't bother moving out of my way.

Ha.

I go to move around him, and he shoots an arm out to stop me.

"Alaska?" he asks. I'm not sure if it was a question, but that voice.

Why does it do something to me?

I'm used to hearing all kinds of men speak. After all, it's what I do for my other job.

But his voice…

"We asked for you. Serve us!" He strides off, looking back over his shoulder before he gets back to his table. The tables have some privacy, but not a lot. They have a full view of the dance floor and small separators in the middle, with steps that lead to where they are seated. His table is about three away from my main table, and from a side view, I guess he could see me from where I was.

Managing to paste a pleasant expression on my face, I make my way to his table. Louise is already standing there, trying to pour them drinks, but none of them are paying her any attention. I grab the bottle from her, and she blows out a relieved breath, then leans up and kisses me on the cheek before she turns and runs off.

Yes, she fucking runs.

"Are you fucking her?" the man with green eyes asks when I turn to face him. Standing directly in front of him, I see he still doesn't have a glass, so I pick one up and hold it out to him.

"Take it." He does as I say, and I pour him a shot over the ice. He watches me, not moving the glass and not saying another word, as he waits for me to reply to his fucking question.

I'm not sure I should.

He's a customer, and I lie to them to get them to tip me well.

Now, some customers would be turned on by the fact I could be sleeping with a woman. This one, though, scans me as if he wants the truth, and he seems to be someone who always gets the truth no matter the cost.

"Will that be all?" I ask him, not answering his question but standing as close as possible, bent over with my tits in his face. And I have some great tits. But not once do his eyes stray from my face.

"Are. You. Fucking. Her?" he asks again.

I straighten and stare down at him. "The possibility is there," I add with a wink before turning to the other men, who are all watching on intently. I glance at their drinks, note they are still full, and then I spin on my heel to leave to check in on my other customers.

"Are you lying?" he asks.

I stop stock still on the stairs and glance back over my shoulder at him.

"You don't tip well enough to get an answer." I walk off, feeling like pressure lifts of my chest.

That was intense. I keep thinking it but it's true.

He is intense.

Entering the back room, I go straight to my locker and lean against it.

It's been a few hours, and I'm ready to go home. Reaching into my bra and clasping it, I pull out my tips and count the bills.

Fuck.

Only that one-hundred-dollar tip tonight.

Usually, by this time, I'd have an easy five hundred.

Louise owes me fucking big time.

"You can have my tips." I gaze up to see her stride in. She holds out her money, and I shake my head.

Louise only has this one job.

And she needs the money.

"It's fine. I'm fine. Keep your tips. But that's the last time I do you a favor with tables," I warn her.

She nods and bites her lip. "I'm sorry, okay?"

"It's just money. I'll make more later."

"I still feel bad."

I put my hundred dollars into my locker and wave her off. "Come on. Table one is getting gropey. Hopefully, I can get another hundred dollars from him." I wink and march back out.

"Let me take it, and whatever tip he gives, I'll give it to you." I nod as she saunters past me and straight to my booth. I watch as Mr. Handsy grabs her ass and tips her a hundred-dollar bill before he whispers in her ear. She shakes her head, but he keeps on trying to grope her, and I can tell now she's uncomfortable as she attempts to pull away. He doesn't even care.

Stalking up to the table, I push my way between them and look Mr. Handsy straight in the eye. I would call him Mr. Stinky, but I'm trying to be a better person, so Handsy will have to do. Louise stands behind me as I pat his shoulder.

"What drinks you after now?" I smile at him, and one hand goes around my waist as he pulls me to him. I feel his tiny cock, which is hard, touch my belly, and I try not to be sick at the thought.

Disgusting.

"Come home with me. I'll tip you again."

"That's a no, sir. Now, what I can get you is any drink you desire." I go to pull away again, and he keeps me in his arms. Just as I'm thinking of kicking him in the balls, his hand is off me, and he cries out in pain, rocking back.

"She asked you to… *remove… your… hand*." Mr. *I like to dress in all black and ask you weird questions on top of being a total babe* is tightly gripping my customer's hand.

"Let him go," I tell him.

My customer, who is clearly drunk, starts swearing, but the man pays no attention as he stares at me while holding Mr. Handsy's arm in a vice-like grip.

"Do you want me to break his hand?"

"No. Now drop it." My mouth hangs open in surprise, especially when he does as I ask, and the groping dude pulls his hand to his chest.

"Fuck! I was only having fun with her. What does it matter to you? She's a whore anyway." I watch as Mr. *I like to dress in black* turns his focus on my customer. He steps toward him with nothing but venom in his eyes. A smart woman would never get in the way of a man who can glare at someone like that—as if he could kill you in the blink of an eye.

Maybe he can for all I know.

I quickly put myself between them and touch his chest, tapping it with my hand. "Come on, big man, let's get you a drink and back to your table."

His eyes flick to me, and he steps back. "You will *not* come back over here again." I huff at his words, and he locks eyes with me and leans in, growling. "Or I will kill him for touching you."

Ah, what?

His words shock me.

To the damn core.

So much so that I stare at him, speechless, like some school girl.

"Zuko, come on, man. Let's drink. We're celebrating," Grayson says.

Zuko.

It can't be.

Can it?

But how many other people have that name?

It's unique, right?

Zuko steps back again and goes to leave, and I follow, watching him from behind as he walks to his table, but I keep heading straight to the bar.

What are the odds that he could be the same Zuko who calls me?

Slim, right?

I mean, he could live anywhere in the world.

So what are the chances we live in the same city?

And are now in the same room?

Slim?

Shit.

Is that my Zuko?

And then I remember *that voice.*

And it all makes sense.

He *is* him.

And he doesn't realize it's me.

And all I can think is thank fuck for that.

FIVE

Zuko

"WHAT IS WRONG WITH YOU? Why the fuck would you get involved in that shit?" Kyson asks, shaking his head, as I watch her walk to the bar. "Fuck, just go down there and tell her you want to fuck her already."

"Shut the fuck up."

She comes back to our table, holding a new bottle in her hand. Her eyes check everywhere but me as she serves. When she's done filling the glasses of the other guys, she leaves without even offering me anything.

I watch as she disappears before her friend, the other waitress, comes over.

"Oh, you've pissed her off," Louise says as she steps up and as she goes to pour my drink her face flushes red as she looks down not making eye contact. I stop her by placing my hand over the glass.

"Where is she?"

"Drink?" she asks as she glances around.

"Where is she, and why are you serving me?" I urge her.

"She needs tips, and you guys aren't tipping," she answers truthfully.

"Well, shit," Grayson mutters.

"Send her over." I sit back, holding my glass. "*Now.*"

She scurries off, and not even ten minutes later, Alaska arrives. Her lilac hair hangs down her back, and her eyes, which almost match the color of her hair, stop on me.

"You requested me?" she asks, hand on hip.

"Yes." I pull out my credit card and show it to her. She looks at it, confused, before meeting my eyes again.

"You want another drink?" She takes the card from me.

"No, I don't drink," I reply. She squints suspiciously at the empty glass in my hand.

Kyson drank it. I just took it back so she would serve me again.

"Okay then…" She holds up the card. "What am I meant to do with the card?"

"It's your tip," I tell her.

At first, she says nothing, looking at the card and then back to me.

"It's a black card. Unlimited," she states. "You don't tip with cards."

"I do. Take it. Spend it on whatever you want. It's your tip."

"Zuko," Kyson whisper-shouts next to me.

She smirks and slides the card into her bra, and I watch the sexy as fucking sin movement.

"If you say so." She turns and sashays off without another word.

"You didn't just give her your card as a tip, did you?" Kyson asks.

"I can cut it off once I deem she's spent enough," I tell him.

"And what if she buys a house?" he questions.

"Please. She wouldn't," I reply, shaking my head.

The little one approaches again and smiles at us all.

"Where is she?" Kyson asks.

"Oh, she left for the night. You really cheered

her up." She grabs the empty glasses and takes them back to the bar.

Kyson starts laughing next to me and Kenzo joins in as well. Grayson just stares at me over the rim of his glass with a closed lip smile lifting his brows.

"You got it bad."

"No such thing," I say, standing. "Now, leave a tip. And be fucking generous."

"Fuck, no. I'm keeping my black card, thank you very much," Kyson snaps as Grayson pulls out a few hundred dollar bills and leaves them on the table.

I watch that handsy slob grab his cock as he stumbles to the bathroom.

"Don't do it," Kyson warns from next to me.

"I'll be quick," I reply as I follow grabby hands, and they move toward the exit. I walk straight into the bathroom and lock the door once I'm inside. Thankfully no one else is in here.

He goes to the stall instead of the urinal, and I walk up behind him and pull out my pencil knife and stab him in his carotid artery. Just as fast as I push it in, I pull it out, and he slumps forward, his head hitting the toilet. I step out of the stall, shut the door, and wash my hands before I leave.

He cries like a baby, and it's like music to my ears.

Slimy fucking bastard.

Now, I wonder how much that little ball of trouble will be spending on my card.

SIX

Alaska

"YOU'VE REACHED Sage from You Beat It, We Spit It. First, let's start with your name," I sing the words as I sit down on my new couch.

Gosh, luxury really does cost money.

I'm lucky enough to do this job from the pleasure and safety of my own home.

"Sage."

Damn him and that voice.

"Zuko." I know who it is straight away. And I wonder again why someone like him would be calling a sex line. I mean, I've seen the way he looks, and he is easy on the eyes. I wonder if he has some fucked-up fetishes. Yeah, that has to be it. "I want to ask you something."

"Go on," he rumbles.

I lift my glass of champagne—expensive as all hell—and put it to my lips, taking a sip before I ask, "Why do you call me? Is it because you can't fuck a woman? Or do you have some fucked-up way that you like to fuck women?"

"I can fuck, if that's what you're asking, Sage."

Oh, I love the way he says my name.

Like honey melting over warm toast, so smooth and slick.

Even if it's not my real first name.

"Okay, tell me, then… When did you fuck the last woman? How was it? What did you do?"

"Aren't I paying you to fuck me over the phone?" he replies.

"Let's be real, Zuko. You call to listen to me speak. Do you even touch your cock while I'm talking?"

"Always," he whispers. "But to answer your question, I start by letting my hand roll over the curve of their neck, causing their pulse to become stronger beneath my fingertips. Did you know by putting a knife straight into that same spot, it can kill you in approximately five to fifteen seconds?"

"I did." I smile.

"Good girl. Now, after that, I would lean in real close…" His breathing picks up through the phone, or was that mine? I'm not sure. I take another sip from my glass as I listen to him. "I would ask her if she wants it fast…or *slow*." He draws out the last word. "And I would give her the exact opposite of what she wants because why not play some fucked-up games."

I go to drink more of my champagne and realize it's gone.

"Are you still there, Sage?" he asks.

"Yes," I reply, standing and walking to my counter to pour myself another glass. I'm going to need it…and a vibrator. I go to my room and pull out my vibrator and smile as I lie on my bed with my glass next to me.

"Carry on," I tell him. Turning on the toy, I put it to my clit first because that's the area that makes me come, hard, and I let it do its job.

"Why can I hear buzzing?" he asks.

"Carry on…" I say again. "What would you do next?"

"I'm a mean lover, Sage."

"How mean?"

"I once almost drowned a girl while I fucked her. Would you like me to drown you?"

"If I come, why not," I say as the vibration picks up speed.

"Fuck! Why say shit like that?" he grumbles.

I let a moan slip through the phone.

"I met someone." His admission makes me pause. "And she's fire."

"Enough to burn you in hell?" I whisper back.

"Yes," he replies, and I hang up. Then I turn off my work phone and finish my orgasm myself.

"You invited me out. I didn't think I would see the day," Louise says. She's dressed in a bright fluorescent green dress and pink heels. Weird combo, but she manages to make it work.

"My treat," I tell her, smiling as the waiter approaches.

"This place is flashy. Are you sure you can afford it?" she whispers.

"I can't, but this can." I show her the little black card that I've had all week and have been using every day.

"How did you get one of those?" she asks, her tone laced with awe as the waiter places a napkin on each of our laps. I put the card on the table, and her eyes follow it like she's never seen one outside of work before.

I hadn't either.

"Can I start either of you with some wine, perhaps?"

"Red, please," Louise says.

"White," I add.

He heads off to place our drink order, and she glances back at the card.

"When I get to be a big girl like you, I want one of those." She points to it. "How did you get it?"

"Zuko." I say his name since I know it now, and her eyes go wide.

"Shit. Did you steal it? Please don't steal from them. They will kill you, no joke. Did you hear what happened to the man who was grabby with us that night?"

"Huh?" I ask, confused.

"Last week, when they came in. The guy at your table who was grabby? Well, anyway, he was stabbed in the neck in the bathroom. Someone found him after you left, and the bar was shut down."

Holy shit. It couldn't have been him, right?

Would he?

I mean, he did tell me if that guy touched me again, he would stab him. I just didn't think he would actually carry the threat through.

"Do they know who did it?" I ask.

"Nope. The bar has been closed all week. I know you only work weekends, but shit, it's been hard."

"You need to find another job," I tell her.

"I know." The waiter comes back with our wine, and she smiles as she takes hers.

"Do you think it was them?" I ask quietly as the waiter retreats.

"Yes, but I would never say that to anyone else but you."

"Why?"

"Because I like my head where it is…firmly attached to my body." She smiles.

"They can't be that scary."

"You did see them, right? Were you not intimidated?"

"I was, but then I realized they're just men. And I am a woman, one who can make men drop to their knees. Pussy is where the power is." I wink at her.

"Oh, gosh, I really do have to get used to the way you speak." She giggles.

"Tell yourself your pussy has power, and you shall have power," I advise, holding back the laugh.

The food starts coming out—a seven-course

meal. Each plate seems to get smaller and smaller, but holy shit does it taste better and better with each bite.

"Miss, the owner of the card would like to speak to you." I turn to the waiter, who is holding out a phone to me.

"Oh shit," Louise mutters.

I reach for the phone, and his voice echoes through to my ear. "Alaska." My eyes flutter shut at the sound of his voice. "I see you have been using your tip money well."

"You didn't set a budget," I say, smiling as dessert is served.

"It seems I should have cut it off when you hit the hundred K mark."

I can't help but giggle a little at his words.

"The dress I'm wearing right now cost me $5,000. I would show you and thank you, but you know…"

"I would be careful with whispering things you may not want the answer to."

"Oh, I do want answers. And I'm about to go Victoria's Secret and buy the most expensive bra and panties I can get."

"I was about to cut off the card until you said that. I expect photos," he says before the call is cut.

I hand the phone back to the waiter, who rushes off quickly.

Louise gapes at me. "Are you flirting with Zuko?"

I pick up my glass of wine. "Tell me everything you can about him," I demand, leaning into her.

She picks at her chocolate dessert and shakes her head. "Are you sure you want to go down that lane?"

"I think I'm about to. Plus, I bet he can fuck like a machine." She chokes on her dessert and picks up her wine, drinking it before she shakes her head at me.

"I've only known one girl who has slept with him, and from what I heard, he's a maniac in bed."

"Like?" I raise a brow.

Louise wipes her mouth with her napkin, her pink lipstick coming off.

"She was covered in bruises, but every time someone mentioned them, she just smirked." She rolls her eyes. "Who smirks at pain?"

"Someone who clearly got off."

"Oh shit…" Her eyes lift to a spot over my shoulder, and when I spin around, I see exactly why she just swore.

Zuko is striding directly toward me.

And if I were a sane woman, I would run.

Far, far away.

But instead, I sit and cross my legs as he nears us.

"Ladies," he drawls, his eyes locked on me. "I see you are enjoying the meal I paid for."

I raise the glass. "We are. Care to join us?"

"I think I'm going to leave. Thank you, Alaska." Louise stands, steps up beside me, and kisses my cheek before she glimpses back at Zuko. "And thank you for paying." She giggles before she scurries off. He doesn't wait a second before he takes her seat directly across from me.

"Have you come to collect your card?" I ask, smirking.

"No, actually."

I raise a brow at his words.

"So why are you here?"

"I came to see the dress you're wearing since it cost me a *lot* of money."

I pull the chair out and stand. Taking two steps, I stop directly next to him and turn in a slow circle, showing him every angle. When I finish, I make to go back to my seat, but his hand flies out and catches my wrist, effectively stopping me.

"I didn't see clearly enough. Spin again." His

words send shivers all over my body, and I feel the goose bumps take over, but I listen to him and do as he says, turning slowly. When I face him once more, after his eyes have burned right through my dress, I find him licking his lips. "Do I make you nervous?"

"Why would you think that?" I ask.

"Because your breathing changed, and that only happened when I arrived."

I take my seat and sit back down.

"I wouldn't call it nervous."

"Oh? What would you call it?" He smirks, leaning back in his seat. The confidence he shows is flying off him in waves of utter domineering assertiveness.

The waiter comes over and offers him a glass. He waves him off and doesn't take his eyes off me.

"Interested," is all I can manage to say.

"The feeling is mutual." His eyes move to my hand. "You aren't married?" he asks.

"Would that matter?" I reply.

He shrugs. "One less person I would have to kill, is all."

Well, fuck.

"Not married," I confirm. "You?"

"Why would I do something so suicidal as to tie myself to a person?" he answers.

"Suicidal. Interesting word choice."

"Yes, I guess it is." His jaw relaxes and he draws in a shallow breath. "I have an errand to run, and I hate errands. Care to join me?" He stands, offering me his hand.

"Can I keep your card?"

"For the time being."

"You must be pretty rich, huh?" I ask, lifting my bag to my shoulder.

"I wouldn't class myself as rich. Rich is crass, wealthy has a better ring to it. Do I have money that I don't spend? Yes."

"Why don't you spend it?" I question as I make my way to the door.

He matches my steps and never misses a beat as he speaks, "Never had anything to spend it on before."

And I get the feeling he is talking about something more than possessions.

SEVEN

Zuko

WHAT A LITTLE VIXEN, that's the only way to describe her.

A fucking vixen.

The way her hips sashay in that dress is driving me insane. I can't tell if she chose the cherry red dress because it matches her manicured nails, or because it hugs her curves like a second skin. Either way, I'm thinking of buying her the same dress in every color just so I can rip them off her body.

"Did you drive?" I turn to ask her.

She bites her lip and shakes her head. "I planned to drink, actually. How soon do we need to be at your errand?" she asks, one of her hands clutching her purse.

"There's no rush. Why?"

"Because I have to pick something up."

"What is it?" She rolls her tongue over her lips as she strolls down the sidewalk, and I leave my car back at the restaurant as I follow her.

"Does this *something* have to do with spending my money?"

Her hair flicks over her shoulder as she peers at me. "Yes. Did I tell you," she pauses for effect, "I absolutely love how good of a tipper you are?" Her eyes glow with mischief. Before I can say anything, she spins and heads toward the BMW dealership.

"Oh fuck," I mutter.

She continues until she gets to the doors of the dealership, where there's a salesperson standing there to greet her.

"How are you today? Are you looking for anything, in particular, today, or can I assist you with something?"

"Actually, that red one right there. I want that," she says, pointing to a BMW Z4.

The sales assistant smiles brightly. I bet that's the easiest sale he's ever gotten.

"No problem. How are we paying for that today?"

"Card." She grins and steps back until she's standing next to me.

The sales assistant nods and goes to get the paperwork.

She turns to me. "This, for sure, will get you a blowjob."

"I don't want a blowjob," I tell her, and she shrugs. I lean in close. "But this will require you to spend the afternoon with me, naked."

She flicks her hair again as those eyes find mine. "Naked?" she asks.

"Yes, not a lick of clothing on you."

"Done. As long as you sign for the car."

"Done. I'll have you naked later."

She sucks in a breath at my words, but I don't allow her time to back out as I stride over to where the sales assistant is standing, and I pay for the car. Once I have the keys in my hand, I find her sitting near the door, messing around on her phone. "I want you to know... This is the most I've ever paid to see a woman naked."

Her lips form a wide, toothy grin. "I want you to know this is the first time someone has ever bought me something." I glance at her clothes, with a brow raised. "That doesn't count. I used your card, yes, but you just went all macho and bought me a car. You may even get to touch me when I'm naked. That's how hot that action was."

"Fuck! What do I have to do to get you to sit on my cock?"

"I'm thinking a nice expensive condo…" She taps her chin.

I dangle the keys in front of her.

"Hurry up. Time is ticking." She takes the keys from my hand and goes straight to the driver's side without hesitation. I watch as she slides into the car and starts it, her manicured hands clutching the wheel. I move around to the passenger side and climb in.

"You like the red?" she asks, noticing me staring at her red-tipped fingernails. "You paid for that as well." She smirks before she takes off. And when I say she takes off, I'm not fucking joking. She drives like a bat out of hell, her foot hard on the damn accelerator.

Now, let's get something straight. Death does not scare me. Death and I are old friends, and I've met him a few times and come close to being a permanent resident. But I've always managed to come back to reality.

But this chick's driving is fucking insane.

I manage to type the address into the GPS before I sit back and clutch the door for dear life.

It takes her minutes, probably seconds, before we arrive at our destination.

She giggles. "Thanks for the car. That was fun," she says, and the thrill in her voice is intoxicating.

I grumble under my breath as I get out, and I thank God for the steady ground under my feet.

EIGHT

Alaska

"WHERE ARE WE?" I ask, glancing around.

It's a warehouse, not one I am familiar with or seen. Zuko gets out and shakes his head as he comes around to the driver's side and pulls open the door.

Why does that one subtle gesture cause flutters in my stomach. I've said this before but there's something about him.

I'm not really sure how to put my finger on it just yet.

It's not just that he's good-looking because anyone with a set of eyes can see that. It's how he carries himself. It's that one single glance from him that contains so much more than he can promise, Or maybe he can.

If he ever does promise things, that is.

He stands there, his sunglasses covering his eyes as he stares down at me. I feel his gaze hot and directed at me. He holds his hand outstretched, waiting for me to take it. I clutch the keys tight, unsure if I should or not. He's patient, though, and doesn't rush me or push me.

A loud honk makes me jump, but he doesn't even seem to notice.

"You can stay in the car if you wish," he finally voices after a few moments when I still haven't moved.

"Who are you?" I whisper, placing my hand in his. He pulls me out and shuts the door behind me, then cages me against the car, his arms on either side of me. He leans forward, and his breathing tickles my neck as he takes a deep inhale and whispers, "Whoever you need me to be."

I laugh.

I can't help it.

Who even says something like that?

He ignores my laugh. For long moments he doesn't move, and then his lips smash into mine and he kisses me, effectively cutting off anymore thoughts of laughter.

At first, I don't kiss him back. His body is pressed against mine, and I can feel every inch of him all over me. The outlines of the hardness of his body. The strength ever-present in his lean muscles. *Does he even have an inch of fat on him?*

I'm jealous.

I know I have a little extra cushioning—this girl right here loves sweets. Brownies, cheesecake, you name it, I love it. And right now, he tastes like my favorite cake.

A big slice I want to devour, so I do.

A single, loud honk comes from somewhere nearby, but neither of us pays it any real attention. My hands reach out and grip the sides of his dress shirt, clinging to it as he presses in closer. And now I can feel a different type of hardness, and it's pushing on all the right areas.

Fuck me.

How can he do this to me?

Another honk, but this time it's more persistent. Louder. And it won't stop.

He swears, his lips still bruising mine, as his tongue, which was devouring mine, pulls back. I notice his lips are a darker shade of pink as his body leaves mine.

"Fucking shut up, Kyson." He steps back from me fully and stalks away without even a backward glance. I stand there, stuck to the car, unsure of how to even function.

That was, without a doubt, the best kiss of my whole damn life.

From a man I barely know.

Who just so happens to be filthy rich—sorry, wealthy—and has given me so much already.

With only one ask.

No one has ever treated me the way he has.

"This your new plaything," the other voice says, loud enough for me to hear. "Hope she can swim." He chuckles. When I check over my shoulder to where they are standing, they're both watching me. Intently.

Managing to get myself together, I stand taller and step over to them. "Swim?" I ask.

The newcomer, Kyson, who I saw at the bar, smirks. "Yes, our boy Zuko here has a habit of drowning his fucks."

"That was one time," Zuko grumbles, then looks at me. "She lived. I gave her mouth-to-mouth. She appreciated it." He still has his sunglasses covering his eyes, so I don't know if he winked at me or not, but I have a feeling he is *not* that type.

"I can swim," I say to Kyson. Then I turn to Zuko. "Are we fucking anytime soon?"

"Naked, remember," Zuko reminds me, not even caring that his brother can hear us. "I didn't get you a condo," he adds.

"Speaking of," Kyson says and hands Zuko a piece of paper. I take no notice as they start to move to the trunk of his car. I stay where I am as it opens, and they start talking. Two shovels are thrown near my feet, and I step back in my designer heels as I stare down. "What the?"

"Does she not know who you are?"

"Kyson," Zuko growls.

Kyson shrugs and grins. "I think she should."

Right now, I should be terrified.

It's a normal reaction, right?

To want to run the other way.

I mean, I'm alone with two men in the middle of nowhere, with nothing close by but an old, rundown warehouse. And for reasons unknown to me, they have shovels.

They could do anything to me.

And I was stupid enough to come out here with Zuko and not think anything of it.

"Oh, she looks scared," Kyson notes. "You know how to dig?" he adds.

"What?" I ask, confused.

"Dig." He nods to the shovels.

"Why the fuck would I dig anything? Do you see this dress?" I ask heatedly, pointing to my incredibly expensive designer brand dress. "No way am I getting it dirty."

Zuko's mouth twitches at my words.

"You should tell her who we are," Kyson says to Zuko.

"I'm good. I don't want to know."

"You aren't the least bit curious about how we earn our money?"

"Nope, as long as I get to spend it, I couldn't care less," I reply, with more confidence than I feel.

"That dress you're wearing, that car you're driving, are paid for by greedy billionaires who want their competition killed."

"And?"

"Who do you think did the killing?" Kyson smirks evilly.

I watch Zuko and wait for him to tell me Kyson is joking.

He doesn't.

"I don't care, and I'm leaving now." I turn around and start walking back to the car. I hear a loud thump and try not to check what it is as two more blacked-out cars pull up. I stop halfway to the car as someone gets out. Neither of the men I was just with even look my way as they reach into their trunk, pull something out that appears a lot like a body bag, and hand it over. I watch as Kyson grabs the shovels and issues them to the men. Then all eyes turn to me. I freeze, unsure if I should move or stay still.

I see Zuko's mouth move before everyone's focus turns back to him. But even with the glasses on, I know his eyes are still on me. He says something, and before I know it, he's coming my way. Finally, I make my feet move, but as I get to the driver's side door, he shakes his head and holds out his hand.

"I'll drive," he says.

I pass him the keys and walk quickly around to the passenger side. He pushes the door open from the inside before he reaches over me as I sit down and grabs my seat belt. It slides over my chest, and he pulls it tight, so it cuts into my waist.

"Can't have you escaping now, can we, Trouble?" He smirks and buckles me in, lingering longer than necessary before he pulls away and places both hands on the wheel, then drives off.

I don't check behind me. I look down at my hands. My whole body feels like it's shaking on the inside, but my hands are so steady I could probably do brain surgery. I've already established I don't really care what Zuko does for a living. If I'm honest he doesn't really look like a CEO or broker, but I do want to know. I pin my gaze on him. "What do you do?" I ask.

His fingers tap the steering wheel, and I get the idea he won't answer me, but then he says, "I'm a hunter."

"A hunter?" I'm somewhat confused by his answer.

"Yes, exactly that."

I nod. Right, that makes more sense—he hunts wild animals. Is that what that was? I wonder what animal was in that bag. He reaches into his pocket and pulls out a card. When he holds it out to me, I take it and then scan the wording.

"A condo," I say looking at the picture on the card.

He smirks. "Your very own."

"I'm confused. I said I wouldn't sit on your cock until I got a condo, you think this," I hold up the card, "is a condo that counts as payment?"

"Yes. You didn't specify the condo had to be a physical place. So your condo is the picture. Now, where can we go so that I can fuck you?" This time he does look my way. His sunglasses tip down, and I see the raised brow as his lips set into a thin line.

"Is that all you want to do? Fuck me?"

"Yes."

"And that's all? Nothing more after this?" I ask.

"Do you mean will I want to fuck you again, Trouble?" He scrapes his teeth along his bottom lip as he stares at me.

"Yes."

"Yes. I need to fuck you from my system." His brows slide up his forehead as his eyes dance with mischief.

"You're a charmer. Just what every girl wants to hear," I mumble. I see his mouth fighting a smirk, and he shakes his head.

"Where do you live?" he asks.

"Nope. You want to fuck? You're getting a hotel room. You are not welcome in my home."

"Who is welcome in your home?"

I turn to him. "My husband. If I'm lucky enough to get married."

"You want to be married?" He glances my way again as he changes lanes.

"Yes, when I've done all the things I want to do."

"And what all do you want to do?"

"Whatever the fuck I want." My hand falls to my lap as the car slows, and he pulls up in front of the Four Seasons. He hands the keys to the valet as he gets out. My door is opened, and the valet nods to me as I slide out. Zuko waits for me on the sidewalk as I stroll around to meet him. He steps up to the registration desk and hands them another black card, and we are told a room number.

I wonder what sex with him includes.

Will he be rough?

And why the fuck did I agree to any of this?

How stupid am I?

Oh, that's right, I'm horny. And my vibrator just isn't cutting it the way it has for the last few years. I need the heat of a body.

A hot body.

The elevator dings, announcing its arrival, and we both get in it. Neither of us says anything, but I can feel his eyes all over me. Tracing my body and waiting for me to turn to look back at him. I focus on the floor indicator, and when it comes to ours, I don't move. His hand finds my lower back, and he leans over my shoulder, his breath tickling my ear.

"Step out."

My feet move at his command, his hand hot on my lower back as I go.

"Where did that confidence go?" he whispers into my ear, his front hitting my back as he urges me closer to the door.

I'm not sure where it went—*out the front door* is all I can think of because I am a confident person, sassy, ruthless, and independent. But this man makes me feel vulnerable. And weirdly, sexy too. I'm not going to lie, it's a nice change to not be the one in control. It's heady and a huge turn on.

Huge.

"Cat got your tongue?" He puts the keycard to the door, and my hands reach out to stop myself from moving forward, but the door opens, and his breath tickles my ear. "Trouble, Trouble, Trouble…" He steps in, and I follow. The door swings shut behind us, and I manage not to jump at the sound of it closing.

Damn, I'm hyper aware.

While I take a moment to get my breathing under control, I scan the lush hotel room. Damn, he spared no expense just for a room to fuck me in. I would've been okay with a standard room and a queen bed. This looks like a luxury apartment. Two elegant wingback chairs in a deep purple two shades deeper than royal purple compliments the contemporary light gray studded couches. Egg-shell drapes blow in the warm breeze whispering through the white-paned windows open to a terrace with a panoramic view.

I step into the bedroom and gasp at the French blue walls with a cream and bronze Damask wallpaper behind an oak four poster bed with sheer curtains tied to each pole by velvet ropes. Zuko walks to the bed, sits down, and kicks off his shoes. Then he leans back and flicks a look to his crotch then to me. "You owe me if I remember correctly." He motions to the card still in my hand. "I got you a car and a condo."

I can't help the laugh that bubbles up from inside me.

This man in front of me sees no humor in his words, he just sits there resting back, waiting for…

Me?

I'm not even sure what. But it's a time for me to take advantage of what's essentially laid out on a silver platter.

NINE

Zuko

SHE'S A FIRECRACKER.

One I want to put out with my mouth.

Her eyes soak in every piece of me as I sit on the bed.

Who is this woman?

And why the fuck is my cock so hard from simply staring at her?

She still has that red dress on, the one that was paid for by me. She seems to have regained her composure as she steps out of her heels and reaches for the zipper of the dress. But as she does, she turns, giving me her back. And what a fucking marvelous back it is. She undoes the side zipper, and I watch as the material floats to the floor.

I would pay a hell of a lot more than the thousands I did for that dress any day if I get to have this view.

Fuck, when did I get so needy over a damn woman?

I sound like a bitch.

"Turn around."

She ignores me.

Of course, she does.

That's the type of woman she is, after all.

Headstrong.

Willful.

A spitfire.

It's also why she still has my credit card.

"Do I owe you?" she purrs, peering over her shoulder at me, her ass and back in full view. But she's hiding her front from me.

"Owe. What a peculiar word that is. I would call it an agreed-upon arrangement."

"Who will be benefiting from it?" she asks, standing there in nothing but a G-string. She turns to face me, her hands covering her tits and her little red lacy number just barely covering her pussy.

Fuck! My cock is straining against the zipper of my pants so hard.

"I would think we both will," I inform her.

"You think you can make me come?" she asks, throwing her head back and laughing.

I sit there confused and unable to take my eyes off her body.

I'm not a religious man, but I feel like getting on my knees and worshipping her right here and right now.

Every single part of her.

"What's amusing you?" I ask.

Her long neck lifts, and she brushes her lilac hair back off her shoulders. I lick my lips at the motion. Her other arm remains across her tits, covering them but pushing them up at the same time.

Those perfect fucking tits.

"That you think you can make me come?" She smirks.

"Has a man never made you come?" I sit up a little straighter, leaning in and waiting for her to answer. *Is this some sort of dare?* Her arm drops, and her hand goes to her hip.

Well, fuck.

They are perfect tits.

I lick my lips again as she answers me, "No, but they've tried. I usually fake the orgasm to get them to hurry up." She taps her finger to her lips. "I wonder if I'll have to fake it with you too."

"I'll know if you're faking it," I tell her.

Standing, I undo the buttons of my shirt, removing and placing it on the bed. Then I reach for my belt and pull it off slowly, keeping my eyes trained on her.

"I'm not fucking you without protection, just so you know."

With those words, I grin and reach into my pocket, grabbing the condom and placing it between my lips as I raise a brow at her. Undoing my pants, I kick them off. And then I'm standing in front of her, naked as the day I was fucking born.

But with a bigger cock.

And a lot more stamina.

Her gaze falls to my cock, and her tongue darts out and licks her bottom lip.

"I will make you scream," I warn her.

"It's good to have high hopes."

I step forward, the condom now in hand, and reach for her hip, pulling her forward so our bodies touch.

"No hopes needed, just skill." I turn her around, and her hands grab my shoulders as I throw her back onto the bed. She bounces, her tits jiggling, and she giggles.

"That's some real skill, throwing women around."

"You should see what I do to the ones I don't like."

She arches a brow at me. "You like me?" she ponders. "What do you do to the ones you don't like?"

"I don't let them come." My eyes meet hers as I grab her thighs, my fingers digging into her creamy skin. I have to be careful not to bruise it.

But I wonder…

I shake that thought from my head straight away.

"Do you plan to drown me?" She licks her lips and opens her legs a little wider so I can get an even better look. "Or do you have something else in mind?"

I groan at the sight of her. "Depends how much you piss me off." She rolls her eyes, and I reach down for my pants and pull out my knife.

Her eyes go wide when she sees it, and she says, "Don't you fucking dare."

"Who comes to a hotel room with a stranger?" I ask her, my eyes soaking her in. "Didn't your mother teach you not to go home with strangers, even if they flash you their money?" She tries to get up, but I move the knife, so it touches her thigh. She freezes, staring at where the blade kisses her skin. "I like it when they're terrified, can't you tell?" I look down at my cock, and before I can say anything, she screams.

TEN

Alaska

HIS HAND SHOOTS OUT TO cover my mouth as I'm trying to scoot back up the bed. I bite his hand hard enough to taste blood, but he doesn't seem to care. He simply stares at me with those eyes that are impossible to read.

Forest green in color.

How stupid am I?

I mean, let's be real. I was pretty damn stupid, but money makes me stupid.

Argh.

My eyes find the knife still pressed to my leg. If I move, it will slice me. Even now, I can feel it digging in, ready to cut.

He showed me who he was.

And I didn't care.

Yet here I am, naked in a hotel room while he stands in front of me, just as naked as I am, smirking and holding me to the bed with a fucking knife.

The real issue I am having, though—and it's a big one, really big—is that I'm a little turned on.

Make that a lot, actually.

Fuck.

He licks his full lips. It's funny. I'd pay to have lips as thick and full as his, yet I know his are natural.

His eyes leave mine and scan downward. "If you scream again, I'll cut you. Do you understand?" He says it while applying a little pressure to the knife, where I feel the blade breaking the skin. I try not to wince, but I can't help it. "A little blood never hurt nobody." As he says it, he smiles. Removing his hand from my mouth, he slides it between my breasts until it reaches my lower belly.

I follow the movement, both worried and fascinated.

Worried that he will cut me and I'll bleed to death.

Fascinated by what he's doing.

I'm fucked-up.

This is fucked-up.

His hand slides lower, and my body betrays me and breaks out in goose bumps, which he doesn't miss as he reaches my pussy. Two fingers slide along my lips, and when they do, he can tell. He knows. It's the slight twitch of his lips that gives it away. He pulls his fingers away and quickly brings them to his lips, and smiling as he slides them into his mouth, his eyes never leaving mine.

"Little Miss Trouble likes to play dirty."

"How do you know it's not from earlier?" I bite back.

"Oh, it's not."

He's right.

It's not.

He lifts the knife from my leg and slides it toward where his hand was between my legs. A small amount of blood trails in its wake along my skin.

I freeze, my whole body locking up tight.

He notices, and his expression turns wicked.

"Are you finally afraid?" he asks.

Fucking hell, I don't dare look at him. Instead, I stare down at that knife where it rests near my pussy.

That's an area where I'd prefer not to have a knife, thank you very much.

"Little Miss Trouble. What if I…" He moves the blade a bit, and now it's so close that if he moves it any farther, it will slide straight over my most sensitive body part.

"Get that fucking knife away from there, you sick sadist," I shout as I move my hand, careful not to move my lower body, and reach for his cock. I'm sitting up straight now with him hovering over me, our lips close and my hand on his hard length. "If you even think of moving that closer, I will *fuck you up*." I groan as his other hand moves and slides between my folds. He slips one finger inside me, and the knife lowers to the bed.

He slides his finger out and back in, and his cock jumps in my hand. I go to release my death grip on him, but as I do, I see the knife move, and so does my hand. Reaching as quickly as I can, I grab his balls and tug down, all the while squeezing them as hard as I can.

He groans. And when my eyes meet his, I see a mixture of pain and pleasure blazing back at me.

"You like that," I say and do it again. "Throw the knife away, *now*." I growl out the words, and he does so at my command. I pull one more time, gripping tight before I release him. When my hands are back at my sides, he pushes down hard on my chest.

Lowering me to the bed. And before I can see what he's doing or tell him to fuck off, his mouth is on me.

Down there.

Hot and wet.

Most men lick, and lick, and lick, and keep on going in the hopes they are doing it right. Listening for cues on what's working and what is not.

Not Zuko. Nope. He knows exactly what he's doing with his mouth. Very much so.

Each lick and taste are calculated.

And I hate it as much as I love it.

I hate that I am in bed with this man.

That I am enjoying every second of this with him.

And I love that I'm feeling every single part of me come alive.

Asshole.

His tongue is slow and deliberate, building up pace in the exact right spot. Just as I start to move my hips, I feel something hard at my entrance, but I can't lift my head to check. He's right. He *will* make me come. I feel it already.

The only thing that can make me come is my vibrator, and I love her a lot, that is until she stopped making me come.

Lick, stroke.

Lick, stroke.

That's his rhythm, and he doesn't speed up as my hips start thrusting to meet him stroke for stroke, lick for lick. He doesn't stop. No, his other hand comes down on my lower belly, holding me there as he continues his torture. And what a wonderful torture it is.

My hands find my hair, and they start to pull handfuls of my locks from all the sensations running through me.

Fuck.

Fuck.

I hear his manic laugh as I squeeze my eyes shut, and when I come, he slows down even further and continues doing what he's doing as I ride the wave.

He made me come.

With his mouth.

And I didn't have to fake it.

He pulls his mouth away and stands, but I still feel him in me. I'm confused, and when I sit up and check between my legs, I see the sharp end of the knife and the handle inside me.

"I'd suggest you don't move," he drawls as he slides on a condom. His crystal green eyes find mine as he crawls back onto the bed, his hand pushing his hair back that has fallen into his eyes as he does. He lifts my chin, bends down, then kisses my lips, softly. "Told you I could make you come."

I don't say a word.

Fuck, I don't move.

I stay still as a statue.

"Now I plan to make you scream," he says as he reaches between my legs and slides out the knife, blade first so that means the handle was inside of me. He smirks while holding the handle, which is covered in my juices and locks his eyes on mine. "What's up, Trouble? Cat got your sweet tongue?"

I move back on the bed, scooting to the other side.

He grips the knife in his hand, and I wonder what the fuck I'm doing.

Am I that fucked-up that I find this sexy as fuck? Yes. The answer is yes.

But there is a small part in my brain that knows this is all kinds of wrong, and that this man in front of me is not right.

I should run.

Fuck it! That's what I intend to do as I reach for the bedsheet, gripping and pulling it from the mattress, then tying it around myself.

"Trouble?" he asks in a manic voice as he steps around the bed to me. I jump onto the bed, holding the sheet tight reaching for what clothes I can, as well as my bag, then bolt for the door.

As soon as I pull it open, I run, sheet and clothes in hand, not worrying about anything but getting away.

That's the smart thing to do, but no one said I was a smart woman. I never claimed to be, but right now, I know I have to run.

The doorman of the hotel looks at me, shocked. So I pull the sheet tighter around me and get into the taxi that's waiting out front, thankfully.

I rattle off my address and don't dare look back.

ELEVEN

Zuko

"LET ME GUESS. SHE RAN." Kyson laughs as I sit across from him at the round mahogany table. He has a glass in front of him that he isn't touching. His leg starts bouncing while he smirks at me. If he wasn't my brother, I would hit him. Fucking hard.

Kenzo says nothing as he sits next to Kyson, just observing like he does best. If I wasn't in a mood, I might find it amusing that we're all sitting on ornate white chairs trimmed with gold that look like they came out of a fucking Victorian movie. They must be the real deal because the dainty as fuck legs isn't buckling under our weight. Who booked this place anyway.

"She ran," I confirm.

"You didn't try drowning her, did you?" He raises a brow at his question.

"Nope."

"So what did you do? They all want a piece of you till they find out how crazy you are."

I grin, thinking about how hard she came, the way her back arched and her eyes squeezed shut. It's been a few weeks since that night, but Kyson hasn't asked about it until now.

"None of your goddamn business."

"Aw, come on, you always tell."

"Not about this one."

"She did seem a little crazy. Maybe that's what you need… Someone crazy like you."

I don't respond.

There is no need for any more words.

I don't always share what's happening in my life with my brothers. They may be ruthless and the most loyal of fuckers to ever have existed, but some things I keep to myself.

Like Sage…

Standing and walking away, I take my phone with me. Kyson yells out as I leave, but I pay him no attention as I close the door behind me and go straight for the bed. We're in a different hotel tonight with a new job at hand.

We don't take a lot of jobs anymore, but when we do, we get paid a substantial amount. And when I say substantial, I mean in the millions.

We're worth it.

We will hunt down your prey when no one else can.

Then we *will* kill them.

And the body will never be discovered unless it's required. We hardly ever outsource. A few know of what we do, but those who are informed would take it to their grave. Grayson is one of those men. He owns a club full of people fucking, some would call it a promiscuous club, a place full of desires, but I like to keep it simple, it's a sex club. He grew up with us and came from the same neighborhood. And he's almost as fucked-up as us because of it. *Almost*.

Pressing call on my phone, it rings three times before I hear her sexy voice. "You've reached Sage from You Beat It, We Spit It. First, let's start with your name."

"Zuko."

I hear her breath suck in on the other end at the mention of my name.

It's been a few weeks since I called her.

And how I have missed her sweet sexy voice.

"I thought you would stop calling," she says.

"Do you want me to?" When she doesn't reply after a few moments, I ask, "Have you missed me?"

"I don't know." I hear the surprise in her voice. "Have you missed me?"

"I've been thinking about another woman. Would you consider that cheating? That it's her who I want to bend over right now and fuck."

"So why did you call me?"

"Because I like to hear you come." And I tell no lies. I do, very much so. I'm pretty sure she uses a vibrator on the other end of that phone, and her voice picks up and gets harsher as she comes. "Can I text you?" I ask. "If I want to call and can't, can I text?"

"The same rates still apply," she states. "Regardless of text or call."

"I don't care about the cost." I growl out the words becoming impatient. "If I paid you enough, would you send me a picture of yourself?"

"Depends on the price."

The door bursts open, and Kyson stands there dressed in his usual black suit. "Get the fuck up, it's go time."

"Who was that?" she asks.

"I'll text you," I tell her, then end the call.

"You found him?" Kyson nods as Kenzo rolls up his sleeves showcasing his arms which are covered in ink before he opens his phone, typing out something, barely looking up at us as we leave.

"Pops said yellow shirt," Kenzo replies. When he does finally lift his gaze, he mutters, "Found him," as he slides his phone into his pocket.

"He's been hiding from us. It's been a long time." Kyson sneers.

"Six months. Did he really think we wouldn't find him?" Kenzo relays as he slides his gun into his waistband at his back.

As we step outside, two ladies stroll by us, giggling.

Kyson smiles at them, always the ladies' man.

The night breeze is cooler this time of year, and some wear jackets, while others opt to wear jeans or long pants. All three of us are dressed in black from head to toe. It's not because we prefer the color—it's solely because it's harder to see the blood.

Blood likes to splatter.

Blood likes to stain.

If I wore a white shirt, as I have once before, blood is a bitch to get out. It lingers where it's not wanted. And I would end up throwing that shirt out.

Doesn't help I can't wash my clothes to save my life.

But black, well, it's easier. It's also better for blending in. And then, as the years went on, our wardrobe just consisted of black for convenience.

Killing isn't just a sport. It's a way of life for some, and no matter how dark and fucked-up it is, some of us are born to do it.

"Yellow," Kenzo confirms as he and I step into the bar. Ronaldo the hit we have been chasing, spots us as his head turns in our direction. His eyes go wide, and in a flash, he is up and running to the back door. Kyson is already there waiting for him. When we step out into the alley, we find Kyson already has him on the ground, his boot on his bright yellow shirt holding him immobile.

Ronaldo is a runner.

He always has been.

"Come on, boys. Please." It's a plea, but it doesn't faze us. "We're friends. You can't do this."

That is false.

We are anything *but friends*.

Kyson pushes his foot down even harder, and Ronaldo lets off a little scream like the bitch he is. The door to the alley opens, and Kenzo immediately has his gun pointed at some random schmuck who is in the wrong place at the wrong time.

The guy lifts his hands in surrender as he says, "I didn't see anything." He steps back slowly, hands still in the air, as the door shuts in his face.

I bend down and grab a handful of Ronaldo's hair, pulling his face up from the filthy ground. I lick my lips and taste water, and then I lift my face to the sky.

It's about to storm.

Smiling, I glance back to Ronaldo in his bright yellow shirt.

"No more running for you," I tell him.

He groans but says nothing more. I let his head drop, and I move to his legs. Removing my knife, I slice his jeans open as he stays deadly still.

"Don't. Please, don't." He starts to cry like a little baby.

"You ran, Ronaldo. You know better," I tell him.

Kyson is still holding him down with his foot, so he doesn't move. Kenzo shifts to the door and holds it shut so no one else can accidentally come outside.

There are few lights at the back of the bar—it was a stupid mistake on his part to run out here—but it made it easier for us.

"I'll do anything, please."

Ronaldo owes someone a lot of money. Who, I don't know, nor do I care. But that person has the ability to pay for our services and our services he will get.

There is a lengthy process to even get to us. And even then, it's not usually us the client deals with directly. It's Pops; he is basically our finder. Though we do some deals on the side when it pleases us. We don't need Pops, but we keep him around all the same.

"You've run long enough, Ronaldo," I tell him as my knife glints in the moonlight while I reach for his leg and grip his calf. I place the blade on the back of his Achilles tendon and hold him as tight as possible as it slides across his flesh. It's slow, and one of the worst pains you can imagine. The healing process itself is a bitch, but it's best done because Ronaldo, as I said, is a runner.

And now he won't be able to run.

Or possibly breathe.

I haven't decided which one serves our purposes.

We were paid to put the fear of God into Ronaldo, and once he has paid, we will kill him. He just doesn't know that bit of information yet.

But sometimes, just sometimes, we slip and kill them sooner. Well, I wouldn't say slip, considering we don't fuck up. It's not in our nature to do that. It really depends on what mood I am in. And right now, as I lift the knife and look at the crimson blood that stains it, I wonder if it's Ronaldo's time as well.

Should he die tonight, like the scum he is on the dirty cement ground?

Or maybe another day?

Kyson removes his foot from Ronaldo's back and bends down until he is in his face.

Kenzo slides his gun back in place and walks over to his twin.

"You have two days, then we'll be back. You better have paid your dues and said your goodbyes." Kyson reaches for his face and kisses his forehead before he pulls back.

And we all know what that means. He's just given him the kiss of death.

Kyson is going to be the one to kill him.

I remember the first time I saw him do that. He was barely an adult, technically still a teenager. He came to one of my jobs with me. He was talking to the guy, then leaned down and kissed his forehead, whispered something to him before he stood, and smashed his head into the ground with his boot, effectively fucking him up. He finished him off with a shot to the head.

Really, when you think about it, it's all fucked-up shit.

But we love it.

TWELVE

Alaska

HIS TEXT COMES THROUGH, and my body freezes as I see it.

> Show me what you look like.

I stare at that text all day.

I've lied to him about what I look like because it's what I had to do. I told him I have blue hair, and that's obviously not true. Though I have had blue hair in the past, just not right now. Sitting at my table with salad in front of me, I search the internet for the most realistic picture I can find of a woman with blue hair, and then I change the tones of the lighting before I send it to him. Immediately after I click send, I see he's read the message.

What is he doing?

Does he like what he sees?

And what do I care anyway.

It's not me.

The last time I saw this man, I ran from him— as far away as I could possibly get—and it's been weeks since that night. I've spoken to him once over the phone, granted he didn't know it was me, and he spoke about the "real me" to me. It was... *interesting.*

Zuko is someone I should stay away from.

I know in my mind that it's a wise decision, but I just can't seem to get him out of my head.

Not only is he a god with his mouth, but the man also makes my head go crazy with thoughts of him, and a part of me wonders if what he wants to do with me would be enjoyable.

No, that can't be right.

My mind is playing tricks on me.

Good Lord, he put a knife in my damn pussy!

That is insane.

Fucking crazy.

Deranged.

Who does that? Oh, that's right, Zuko does.

I put my phone down when he doesn't respond for a good fifteen minutes, and I wonder what he thinks of *her*. Is *she* pretty to him?

But then my phone dings, and when I check it, I suck in a breath.

> It seems you are a liar. I wonder what else you are...

How could he know that?

There is no way. He can't be that tech-savvy, can he?

I grip my phone, push my food away, and stand as I reach for my bag. I'm wearing a long sweater that covers my work outfit, which I pull on the hem of as I leave to head for my night shift. It's supposed to be a slower night tonight, but that's what Jeff always says. He's a fucking liar, and we all know his games.

When I arrive, I head straight for my locker, pull off my jacket, and stash it inside. I slide my phone into the back of my little shorts and after reaching for my boots, I pull them on. I keep them in my locker so I don't have to walk around in them outside of the bar, unless I'm too lazy and end up taking them home.

"Do you *ever* fucking listen?" I whip my head around to Sarah, who's eyeing my outfit.

This feels like déjà-fucking-vu.

Does this bitch need to get a life or what?

"Fuck off, Sarah."

"You're a dumb bitch, you know that, right," she mutters. This idiot thinks she's in charge because she spreads her legs for Jeff, and thinks she has the upper hand. But no matter what, Jeff won't fire me, and I am not an idiot. Let's face it I make more for his damn bar than any of the other girls. Sarah and Louise probably make the same amount, but they both work more hours than I do. I work the bare minimum to earn what I need, and then I'm out.

"I'll slam your pretty smug face into this locker if I have to. Last warning," I state, shutting the metal door with a loud bang and turning around to face her. Her black hair is slicked back, and her arms are tucked across her chest, pushing up her god-awful boob job. I warned her not to go cheap but like I said, the girl is an idiot. She's applied heavy eyeliner that turns up at the edges, giving her a cat eye look and making her already hard face look harder. Paired with bright red lipstick—she looks like a damn whore.

I hate her.

"You're late...*again*. Not only that, but Louise is also out there serving *your* customers." Her lips pucker as she talks, and it looks like an asshole. Does she ever look in the mirror? Sarah reminds me of someone who has always gotten what they want, and the minute someone else gets more attention, they snap.

I'm that person she wants to snap at, and it seems she is now doing it constantly.

But she also knows it comes with a price.

I won't just sit here and take her bullshit like some people she knows. I will snap right back and worse.

The next time she touches me without my consent—even a tap on the shoulder—I will slam her head into the locker as hard as I fucking can, and I have zero care factor about what damage I do to that face.

She needs to learn manners, and it seems I was put on her path to teach her some.

Sarah continues to stare at me. Her big white

teeth peek through her stained lips when she smirks. God, she gets on my nerves. "Louise can handle them. Now… Fuck off." I sneer at her as I grab a tray and make my way out.

When I step out into the bar, I see Louise in one of the private booths, but this time it's not filled with people. There is only one person, and his eyes have already found mine. Louise follows his gaze checking over her shoulder. A small smile takes over her lips and she relaxes her posture in relief when seeing me. She turns back and says something to him before she steps down the stairs and straight to me.

My feet are frozen to the spot.

The last time I saw this man I ran away from him with only a sheet to cover me. And now he is sitting in my workplace, in a booth that costs a small fortune to book, waiting for me to serve him.

"I'm so glad you're here. He won't buy anything, and I know he's waiting on you." I manage to meet her eyes and nod. She does her usual, stepping into my personal space and wrapping her arms around me as she gives me a quick hug hello. As usual, I don't reciprocate and as usual it doesn't bother her. She's used to that now. "Okay, I'm going to service my own customers now. Let's chat when you finish." She runs off as I stay rooted to my spot.

What do I do?

Do I run again? No.

He doesn't have the upper hand here, I do. Or so I keep telling myself.

I put one foot in front of the other, striding straight past his booth. I feel his eyes burn my body as I pass. I force myself not to look in his direction as I reach the bar and grab some drinks. The bartender waves hello to me, but I can't seem to do the same back. I'm trying to work out the best course of action and how to deal with the man waiting for me.

Being in and out of foster care all my life, I learned early on how to handle men. The system taught me to depend on no one but myself. I can read people's body language and work out how to treat them based on their personalities, so harm never falls on me again.

In one of my houses growing up, they drank —a lot.

They used to hit the kids when they were drunk. And at first, I received those blows, and it was frustrating. Until I learned that if I offered them things, little things to help them while they were intoxicated, they didn't look at me as if I were a punching bag.

It would be as simple as not looking them in the eyes and asking if they want a drink—alcohol, of course. Just helping them as much as possible to view me as a bonus not a burden.

For another family I lived with, it was all in the way you spoke to them. A soft demeanor and a gentle smile would get you food, particularly when it was held back as punishment.

Not all of it was bad.

I was placed with an elderly couple once for about six months. It was the best home I lived in. They cooked every night, and they taught me how to make the best chocolate cake. It's my best party trick, and I made it at many other foster homes when I needed to get on their good sides.

It's a good thing too since it's the only thing I know how to cook.

And it's saved me many times.

Steeling myself, I turn with the tray and make my way to his table. Taking the few steps I need to, I breathe deeply, trying to gain some equilibrium before I glance at him.

"What can I get you?" I ask, noticing all he has is water. "Whiskey, vodka, gin…" I list off a few choices, but he doesn't respond. He quietly assesses me with those eyes that haunt my dreams. "If you aren't drinking, you need to leave," I tell him.

"I paid for this…" He waves a hand around, stopping when it reaches me.

"It's a bar! You get that, right?"

"I do."

"And you don't drink," I state.

"No, though somewhere deep inside, it makes me happy you remember that fact."

I scoff. "Don't let it go to your head. I remember because I spent all your money."

"Do you want to be tipped tonight?" he asks.

"What type of question is that? Of course, I do," I sass, sliding the tray under my arm as I eye him.

"The tip you get will depend on the service, of course."

"I'm not here to play your games *again*." I turn to leave.

"Alaska…" I stop at the sound of my name. My *real* name. "Turn back around and give me those vexing eyes."

Sliding my tongue over my teeth, I turn back to him.

He's leaning forward on the table with a wicked

grin on his lips. "Order a bottle of whatever, send it to a table of your choosing, and charge it to me."

I nod and head to the bar, not stopping to give him an opportunity to speak to me again. When I gain the bartender's attention, I order the most expensive bottle I can find and charge it to his card on file.

Louise skips over and places her tray next to mine. "What did you say to Sarah? She hasn't stopped complaining to Jeff about you." I turn to face her, taking in her bright pink shirt and bouncy hair.

"Sarah can eat my ass," I reply.

She laughs and shakes her head then changes the subject. "Oh…what are your plans for Christmas? My family wants to meet you; I've told them all about you. Are you free, or do you have plans with your family?"

Christmas…

That's the day I get drunk and watch *Home Alone* and pass out on my couch.

It's actually an amazing day and I love it by myself.

"I—"

"No, please come." She raises her hands in front

of her chest in a prayer pose. "Please. Pretty please."

"Fuck, fine." I shake my head.

"You are the best! You can bring a date if you want. Or not." She shrugs. "I'll have all the wine and sweets you want. Thank you again, Alaska." She leans up and kisses my cheek before she happily bounces off again—that girl has more energy than the Energizer Bunny.

I'm not sure why I just agreed to changing my own tradition, but now I'm trying to work out how I can also get out of it.

I prefer time alone.

It's *my* day.

Louise is great and all, but I like being by myself more.

Does that make me self-centered? Probably, but I couldn't care less.

Turning back around, I find Zuko sitting in his booth, fiddling with his phone. I watch as Sarah walks up the stairs toward him and wonder what she's doing. She has on her best fuck-me face, and her hips sway as she walks.

Good, take him.

Maybe you can get fucked with a knife up your pussy too.

I giggle at that thought and quickly shake my head, telling myself that's all kinds of wrong.

Zuko glances up from his phone as Sarah says something to him. She places her hand on her hip, popping it out a little more, as his eyes start to roam. He's not looking at her though. He's scanning the bar as if he's searching for something. And when his gaze stops on me, I know it's me he is looking for. He raises a brow, and how I see that clearly in this dark bar is beyond me, but my heart skips a beat.

I wonder if I should save him.

Or let him be.

THIRTEEN

Zuko

IF ANNOYING COULD HAVE A FACE, it would be this woman in front of me right now. She is talking —I mean, her lips are moving—but I can't hear a word that leaves her mouth. It sounds like gibberish. Instead, my eyes find Alaska's. She is watching the exchange from where she stands at the end of the bar.

"Did you hear me?" the woman in front of me asks.

I grip my phone in hand as I glance back at her. "What did you say?"

"I said you don't need to pay for her services. I can give you a better rate."

"A better rate?" I repeat her words as a question. The music is loud, but I'm not really paying all that much attention.

"Yes, like I said… My name is Sarah." She rolls her eyes as if her pretentiousness will get her somewhere with me.

"I'm happy to pay whatever I'm paying now," I tell her.

She bites her bottom lip as Alaska steps up right next to her. Sarah's sharp eyes fall on Alaska, and she seems to stand a little taller.

"Are you lost, Sarah?" Alaska asks in a bored tone.

"I was just seeing if this customer here would like a better waitress," Sarah says with false sweetness and all kinds of bravado.

"You can have him. He's all yours," Alaska answers, then walks off.

Sarah smiles brightly like she can't believe her luck as Alaska heads back to the bar where she has been most of the night.

"She must really not like you if she was willing to give you up that easily. She never gives me anything," Sarah says, her eyes lit with triumph.

I want to cut her lips from her goddamn mouth.

This bitch is fucking annoying.

"Get her back," I order, waving a hand. Sarah

pales at my words, and her brows pull together so tight they form a single line. "Get her back, or I'll get you fired."

Her hand swings to her hip as a slow grin touches her lips. "You don't have that power."

"You know the owner, then?" I ask.

She opens her mouth to speak but stops, then tries again. "My boyfriend is the manager."

"Okay, so I will have him fired. Now fucking listen and... *Get. Her. Back.* You have ten minutes," I warn.

"Fuck, you're crazy. Hot but crazy." As she storms off, she waves a hand over her head. "You can have your stupid crazy bitch of a waitress. You are *not* worth it," she shouts over her shoulder. I see her stomp up to Alaska, who rolls her eyes when she speaks to her. Alaska spins around and comes straight back to me with no tray in hand.

"Sarah thinks you're crazy, and that's saying something coming from that idiot."

I want to kiss her pink lips. Run my finger over them and hold her in place while I do bad, wicked things to her.

"Stop looking at me like that."

One thing about Alaska, she has more balls

than any other woman I have met. She speaks what's on her mind and gives as good as she gets.

"Like what?" I ask.

"Like you want to eat me," she whispers, but I hear it over the music. I sit back in the booth, draping my arm across the top of the seat as I cross one leg over my thigh. Her eyes track each movement.

"That's because I do," I reply honestly.

"Where is your knife?" she asks, with her chin raised in what seems to be a little defiance.

"Why? Would you like to be acquainted with it again?" I remember how hard she came last time I used it on her.

"No. And if you ever do that again, there will be hell to pay."

She doesn't realize what she just said… "*Ever do that again*." She used "*again*." Which means she hasn't completely run from me.

Not quite yet anyway.

Placing my foot on the floor, I stand, leaning down until I'm in her face. She angles her head up slightly—in her heeled boots she is almost as tall as me. My hand lifts and touches the edge of her cheek. Stroking it, I lean down farther and kiss just below her earlobe.

"Are you wet, Trouble?" I ask. She nods as if she's on autopilot, and I let out a pleased hum at what a good girl she is for me. "Show me where."

She takes my hand that's gripping her waist and moves it. Her little hand wraps around my wrist as she pulls it between us. She steps back just a fraction, so there is room as my hand is pushed onto her pussy.

She has tight little shorts on, and I let my fingers roam before one pushes aside the material and slides up. Her breath hitches and I let my thumb graze her lip as I stare at her. "Be quiet, Trouble. We don't want your customers thinking this is a free service." She blinks at me as my finger touches her wetness. She isn't drenched, but she is for sure wet. If you are watching from a distance, it would appear like we are almost kissing. The side where my hand is in her pants faces a wall, so no one can see as my fingers push in all the way.

"Zuko," she says breathlessly.

"Yes, Trouble?" I move my finger in and out of her while my other fingers rub over the outside of her shorts and over her clit.

"This is…"

"Good?" I finish for her.

She shakes her head, but I lean in and kiss her

lips, not giving her a chance to respond. Her hands raise to my shoulders, gripping and digging her nails into my skin through my shirt.

"So this is why you wanted her back." Alaska freezes at the sound of *that* voice. "I'm telling the boss. You're getting fired, you stupid bitch."

I slide my finger out of her as her eyes find mine. I keep my eyes locked on Alaska's as I speak to the woman behind her. "Tell your boss to come here."

"Oh, you can be sure I will." Sarah sneers, and her contemptuous appearance clearly shows she has no respect for Alaska or me.

Alaska pulls away from me, fixing her shorts into place, and she swings around. "If I get fired…" Alaska gives me an angry glare.

I put my finger to my lips and taste in reply.

She stomps off.

FOURTEEN

Alaska

I'M helpless to do anything as Jeff marches straight up to the private booth after he shoots me a dark glare on his way.

Louise comes to stand beside me and glances at where I'm looking. Zuko is sitting down, his arm is back on the top of the seat, his legs crossed as they were before, as he listens to whatever it is Jeff has to say.

"What's going on?" Louise asks.

"Sarah caught me getting finger-banged by the customer," I tell her.

She coughs, covering her mouth with her hand. "Are you joking?" I raise a brow at her. "Okay, you aren't. Well, shit."

"He has great fingers and knows how to use

them." I shrug and glance back at them, exchanging words.

"Shit! She's going to try to get you fired, isn't she?"

"Yup."

"I don't want to work here if you aren't here."

"You'll be fine," I reply, patting her on the arm.

"Incoming," Louise hisses as Sarah approaches us.

Sarah stops directly in front of me, crosses her arms over her chest, and pops one of her hips out. "You are *so* going to get fired, and this place will be so much better without you."

"Fuck off, Sarah." I growl out the words, turning around and grabbing a tray before I storm off. I feel like I should have a shirt that says Fuck off, Sarah because whenever she is in the vicinity of me, that's all I perpetually say to her.

As I make my way to one of my other tables, Zuko spots me. His eyes track my movements as Jeff stands in front of him and talks. I try to assess their body language, but Zuko exhibits his I-own-the-fucking-world attitude, and Jeff is, well, Jeff—boring and bland with a slight hunch in his back.

After serving one of my other booths, I go back to the bar to drop off the empty tray before I step out back. Jeff isn't far behind me. His black shoes stop when they reach me, and up behind him comes Sarah with a smile so wide on her lips they stretch so much she looks like Julia Roberts as she stands there waiting for... what? I don't know.

A pat on the back.

Praise for doing a good job.

Probably for me to get fired, so she can gloat.

"Your customer..." Jeff says through gritted teeth.

"She's a whore. I told you that. And a terrible employee," Sarah rattles off.

"What about him?" I ask Jeff, totally ignoring her stupid comments.

Jeff turns to Sarah and shakes his head.

"Shut up, Sarah," he snaps.

Her mouth opens in shock. "How can you talk to me like that?" she argues back.

Jeff lifts his hand and slides it through his hair. "Because you are causing me more trouble than you realize," he barks back.

Fake tears start to well in her eyes. "I was doing the right thing. You can't have a whore ruin this bar's reputation. It's been happening since you hired her."

"Technically, that was the first customer I let

stick his fingers in my pussy, and that's probably because he tips like a king." I smile, and both of them whip around to face me.

"See? Do you see what I mean?" Sarah shrieks.

"What?" I say, shrugging my shoulders.

Jeff swears under his breath, and for some reason, her fake tears are gone. That is until Jeff looks back at her.

"You're fired," he whispers, but there is an apology lacing his tone.

We all stand there shocked.

Did he? No. He couldn't have.

Sarah's fake tears are back once again in full force. She swipes at her cheeks hard, and then she slaps Jeff across the face. He winces, and as she goes to do it again, he manages to catch her hand in mid-flight.

"You are fired because that customer you just pissed off has worked for the boss. He knows him, and it was either you or me. And I am *not* losing my job over *you*."

Oh, wow! I did *not* see that coming.

How can Zuko rein that much power?

Enough to get someone fired? That's, well, I don't even know.

Sarah turns to me and raises her hand, ready to

slap me. But I step back, lift my foot, and kick her in the cunt. She screams as she flies backward and lands on the floor. Jeff swears and goes to see if she is okay, but she loses it and starts kicking and hitting him as much as she can.

"Fuck, Sarah! Take your shit and get out." Jeff leaves her on the floor and storms off.

Louise comes up at that moment. "Um… What's going on?" She directs the question at me.

"Sarah got fired because she hasn't learned to keep her stupid slutty mouth shut and stay out of other people's business. Then she tried to hit me, but before she could, I kicked her in her useless cunt and sent her flying backward, where she landed on her ass." I wave a hand in Sarah's direction. Louise looks down at Sarah and offers her a hand, but Sarah slaps her hand away, managing to stand on her own.

"You're a bitch, lowlife scum. You get that, right?" Sarah snarls.

I shrug my shoulders and reply, "It's still better than what you are."

Sarah storms off, and the back door opens again. Zuko is now standing there, filling the space with his large, muscular frame. He reaches out and grabs my hand and pulls me back out to the bar without a word. He leads me to the middle of the dance floor—a place I usually refuse to go—and pulls me to him. He doesn't sway or move, simply stands still with his hands around my waist.

"What are you doing?"

"Making you work for your tip, of course," he replies.

"What if I said I don't want your tip?"

He leans down and whispers in my ear, his hot breath tickling me as he does, "I can give you more than just the tip. I can push all the way in." A shiver racks my body, and I'm pretty sure he feels it as he holds me tighter to him. "Move your hips," he orders.

"I don't dance with strangers," I tell him.

"I'm not a stranger." His hands slide down to grip my ass and pull me to him until there is no air between us. I feel him everywhere. My head rests on his shoulder as we stand there in one another's embrace.

How do we appear to the outside world right now?

Weird?

Funny?

Like we are trying to fuck but don't know how?

Who the fuck knows.

"I hate being touched," I confess.

"No, you don't," he says in my ear.

"I do. I can't stand it," I whisper back to him.

"You liked to be fucked and touched by me."

Dammit! He isn't lying, and I hate that the most. How do I like it? I mean, it's not like we have sat there and cuddled. Ew. I shake my head at the thought of that. I despise being cuddled.

"Now move," he says again.

I bite my lip as I move my hips, swaying slightly from side to side. "How did you get her fired?" I ask.

"I'll answer that when you put your hands around my neck." I do as he asks and lift my hands until they're draped around his neck. When I peek up at him, our gazes lock, and if I were a smart girl, I would move away. But I have never claimed to be smart, and those eyes hold promises of incredibly bad, dirty, and wicked things…

He intends to do to me.

"I know the owner. I've done a job for him."

"What if he had said no?" I ask, and he chuckles lightly.

"No is not a word most people understand when dealing with me." I raise a brow at his words, knowing I have said that word more than once to him. "Except you, of course."

"You can't always get what you want."

He squeezes my ass a little tighter. "Yes, I can. I have what I want right now in my arms." I go to move my hands, but he pulls me closer and holds even tighter. "Do you want me to fuck you, Alaska?" he asks.

"No."

"Let's not start with lies, shall we?" I glance around and notice everyone is busy having fun, and no one is paying attention to what we're doing.

"You're hard," I say, pointing out the obvious.

"I am. I did just taste something incredibly sweet and quite to my liking, actually."

"What?" I ask in confusion.

"Your pussy was all over my fingers." *Oh.* "Move your hips faster." He bends down and kisses my neck, and I hate that every part of my body lights up like an electrical circuit at his touch. I try to move away, but his grip doesn't loosen.

"Zuko."

"Hmm…"

"Remove your hands." He does so, and I turn and walk away. I pass the bar and head to the restrooms. Stepping into the ladies' room, I go straight for the stall. I need to cool myself down. Just as I go to shut the stall door, it's pushed open, and in strolls Zuko, closing it with his back. He leans against the door and turns the lock.

I say nothing, but I do stand there wide-eyed.

What is he doing in here?

I do the only thing I can think of—I reach for my shorts, pull them down, and step out of them, and then I touch myself.

"You remember the rule, right? No glove, no love." I smile as my fingers slide between my folds. His eyes track my movements while his hand pulls out a condom. He undoes his belt and zipper, then pulls his cock free. It's long, hard, and thick. *Fuck, it's beautiful.* As soon as he slides the condom on, he reaches for me and lifts me up, so my legs wrap around his waist. My hands reach for the top of the door, and I hold on as he lifts me higher so I can feel him at my entrance.

I don't need to be warmed up, it's like the build that comes with tantric sex, he has done that all fucking night with his teasing. And now I'm at that point where I'm hungry, all over, for him. The need is so strong that I feel like I might combust from the want.

He goes to speak, but I pull my hand down from the door and slam it over his mouth. A few girls giggle as another pees next to us. He bites my hand, but I don't move it. I feel his grip tighten on my hips as he takes full control. I start moving my hips.

He is right there, if I can just…

Then boom, he pulls my hips down.

I almost lose my hold on the door, and a scream erupts from me as he impales me on his cock. He fills me in more ways than one. I try to gather my breath, but he is moving me up and down in a slow, steady movement that's putting all the right pressure on my clit.

I've had sex before.

I've fucked before.

But this…

This is ecstasy.

The way he hits every notch, every spot, it's perfect.

Fuck that everyone in here probably knows what we are doing.

Fuck that I'm in the women's bathroom fucking a man who last fucked me with a knife.

Fuck it all.

Because as his rhythm picks up, my hands grip the door harder, and my head falls to his shoulder. I bite down hard to stop the scream. He grunts in my ear, and I moan into his shoulder as I come—really fucking hard.

"I want to be fucked like she is," I hear a girl mutter.

Zuko doesn't care what others are saying. He keeps on going and going until I feel myself build again.

No way.

No fucking way.

I pull back and look at him. And when I do, I see something I'm not sure I like written all over his face.

Danger.

For what? I'm not sure.

I get he is a fucked-up man.

Not only with the fucking but in all aspects of life.

He's one of those men you're warned to stay away from, and I've just let him deep inside of me without a second thought, only for my own pleasure.

Was it worth it? Yes, because it's the best sex I've had in my life.

But now I'm afraid I will never be able to escape this man.

Is it really fear in my gut or excitement? I'm honestly not sure.

I never had a mother who told me to stay away

from bad men. I have lived with their kind most of my life.

And all of them wanted me for one reason or another.

What makes this man any different?

"You can't run. I'll find you," he says as another orgasm hits me.

And this time, he slows and smashes his lips to mine.

FIFTEEN

Zuko

"ALASKA, we are down a girl, and I need help." Alaska pulls back from my lips and pushes on my chest. I lift to pull out of her, then place her on her feet. She reaches for her shorts, but not before she sits on the toilet in front of me.

"I'll be out in a minute, just need to pee." I tuck my cock back in and discard the condom.

"Are you really peeing in front of me?" I ask.

"Yes. If you have a problem, leave." She shrugs. I watch as she reaches for the toilet paper and wipes herself before she pulls her shorts up. "You didn't leave."

"No, because I'd like to know all the ins and outs of that sweet pussy," I tell her. "Plus, I can't say I have ever seen a woman pee in front of me."

ll women should pee after sex. I bet you just ___ them out afterward," she says, wiggling her ___orts up all the way and doing up the buttons.

"Yes, very much so. Or they run." I smirk at her.

"Oh, I can only guess why." She rolls her eyes.

"I've been tame with you."

Her eyes almost bug out of her head.

"Tame? Are you joking?" She shakes her head. "You're crazy."

"Making you come is tame, trust me."

"And how else would you make me come?" she asks.

"Do you really want to know the answer to that question?"

She seems to think on it, then says, "I gotta go." Alaska pushes past me and reaches for the door, unlocking it. But I push it closed.

"Let me see you again."

She remains facing the door, but after she says nothing for a beat or two, she finally turns to me. "How else would you fuck me?" she whispers.

"I can show you, but I'm not going to say you'll like it."

"If I can keep the knife in my hand," is her answer.

"Deal," I agree.

"Will it hurt?" she asks.

"Do you want it to hurt?" I whisper closer to her ear.

"Maybe a little." I run my finger over her bottom lip at her words.

"Have a good night, Alaska." I pull open the door to see her friend is still standing there. Her eyes go wide, and I tip my head to her as I saunter out. While the door slowly closes behind me, I hear her friend ask how it was, and Alaska says it was the best sex she's ever had.

When I get to the front to wait for my car, I see the crazy waitress from earlier tonight.

She eyes me and steps over. "I know who you are," she whispers.

My car is pulled around, and the keys are handed to me.

"Good night, Sarah. And by the way, I wouldn't make threats. Those can get you killed." I give her a menacing glare as I climb into the car.

"You are a killer!" she screams. "And I'll prove it."

I take no mind to her stupid words as I pull away.

All I can think about is Alaska's sweet pussy and what I plan to do to it next time.

"Why are you smiling?" Kyson asks the following day as he walks into my place uninvited, as he usually does, to annoy me. Kenzo is nowhere to be seen, which is just like him; he would live out his life quite happily if he never had to interact with another human being again. Kyson is a people person, but only with certain people. "Did you find a woman to fuck and kill?" He chuckles to himself as he opens my refrigerator searching for something but coming up empty.

My house is simple with just the basics—there isn't one thing that's flashy about it and I'm fine with that. It has gray flooring, two black two-seater sofas, and a television hanging on the wall. I have two bedrooms—one houses only my bed, and the other is the computer room.

"I fucked, not killed. I don't kill a woman when I fuck her," I reply, and he raises a brow. "Apart from that one time," I amend, looking away. "That was her own stupidity, and technically I had already come, so we weren't fucking."

"Was your cock still inside of her?" he asks.

"I'm not answering that."

He starts to laugh as he grabs a bottle of water and comes to sit next to me on the couch. I wait for him to speak because I know that's what he wants to do.

"Do you think we would be who we are right now if we had a different upbringing?" he asks.

I turn the television off and face him. "Why are you asking me this?"

He shrugs, lifts his water to his lips, and takes a sip.

"Kyson, if you want out, you say it. You know I would kill anyone who tried to stop you from leaving this life."

"Only Pops would try to have me killed," he says.

He isn't wrong. We all trust Pops to a certain extent, but that's as far as it goes, Pops brought us into this life. He is probably more fucked up in the head then anyone of us, and that's saying something considering how fucked up we each are. So we know to only trust him in certain aspects of life, not all.

"I'd kill him before he could try," I declare and turn back to the television, flicking it on again. I ignore the newscast that comes on as I repeat, "If you want out, you tell me."

SIXTEEN

Alaska

MY PHONE PINGS, Sage's phone. When I check it, there's a picture of Zuko's hand holding a belt.

Now, I'm not one who is usually attracted to certain body parts—I mean, the abs, face, and cock are nice, as well as the ass. But hands, I haven't really thought that much of before. I stare down at the photograph as I sit in the back room of the bar. The night's done, and now every time I walk past the women's restroom, I can't help but smile a little bit.

"What has you smiling?" Louise asks as she sits across from me and puts her feet up on the desk.

"Do you think hands are attractive?" I ask.

"Um… Weird question, but hell, yes. Especially if they're muscly and a few veins pop. Add some plain jewelry, and *boom!* I'm a sucker." She throws a Skittle into her mouth. "Why?"

I bring the photograph up and show it to her.

"Shit, those are some good hands. Imagine them roaming all over your body as they pick you up by your ass and grip it tight."

I check the phone. That's exactly what those hands have done to me. And it did feel fucking amazing. "You look tired. Everything all good?" Louise asks.

"I haven't been sleeping much this week," I tell her honestly.

"Why?"

"Nightmares," I whisper, keeping my head bowed. They don't happen often, but when they do, they come in full force. And it's impossible for me to want to sleep, let alone stay asleep. I thank my second foster home for that wonderful addition to my life.

"Damn, that sucks. Do you take anything for them?"

"Nope." I stand, sliding my phone into my shorts as I get my jacket out of my locker and slide it on before I change out of these boots into some flats. It's early morning now—three a.m.—and I am dead-ass tired. But I know I won't sleep, no matter how hard I try.

"What about drinking? We can drink for what's left of the night, and hopefully, that will knock you out," she offers as I head to the back door. She follows, gripping her bag in her hand.

"I don't know, I just—"

"Alaska," Louise interrupts. "I think someone is here for you." I look to where her finger is pointing and see Zuko leaning against my car. The very same car he bought me. I thought after that night I ran out on him I would never see that car again, yet here it sits.

"Do you want me to stay?" she asks.

I shake my head as I stare at him. He's dressed in all black—his usual attire—as he waits for me.

"Those hands. Now all I'll be thinking about is those hands," she whispers.

I stifle a laugh and watch as she walks to her car, giving Zuko a small wave as she gets in. He doesn't acknowledge her, just simply stares at me.

My shoes crunch lightly against the concrete with each step I take to reach him. When I'm standing in front of him, I stop and look at the car.

"You brought me my car," I say, smiling and tucking a piece of hair behind my ear.

"I don't have your phone number or address, so I figured it was best I return it myself."

"It's still mine?" I ask, confused.

"Yes," he replies without hesitation. I hold out my hand for the keys, and he glances at it. "I want your number. And I want to see you more," he declares.

"See me more?" It's been a week since I last saw him. I like that he isn't needy, but when he wants something, he takes it. Me included. I can't help but stifle a yawn and quickly cover my mouth.

"Are you tired?"

I raise a brow at him. "Of course I am. I just finished a shift on my feet for eight hours straight." He seems to think about my words before he opens the passenger door and indicates for me to get in. "Where are we going?"

"To my place. You need rest." I look at the car and back at him. "I can't sleep," I tell him.

"You can and you will."

"You just want to fuck me again," I say, getting in the car.

"Oh, make no mistake about it, I very much do." He shuts the door and walks around to the driver's side. I watch him as he starts the car and pulls out onto the road. "I will fuck you again. But when you are not a walking zombie."

"I don't sleep well," I admit. Fuck, I blame the lack of sleep on my recent path of honesty—first Louise, now him.

"What helps you sleep?" he asks.

As he pulls onto the highway, I don't even bother checking where we're going. I just turn my body and stare at him—trust me when I say it's a better sight.

"I haven't really figured that part out yet. It's taking me a bit," I share with a shrug.

"I don't understand."

"Some nights I sleep fine, some nights I won't. It's just a matter of when my brain decides it wants to fuck me over, really." His fingers tap on the steering wheel, and I can't help but study them. He has a plain black ring on his right ring finger.

The car seems to go completely silent before his eyes shift my way.

"I slept great that night after you fucked me," I add with a smirk, but he doesn't give the reaction I thought he would. No wide eyes at my words. They just don't seem to shock him as much as they do other people. Even other men, when I randomly blurt stuff out, are usually shocked. Zuko, not so much. He looks at me like he is trying to piece me together.

You and me both, mister.

"Do you want me to fuck you again?" he asks.

"I'm not sure I would be much fun. Plus, that would require touching and as you already know, I hate being touched." I yawn again as we pull up to a one-story house. The outside is dark, so I can't really see all that much, but I can tell the lawn is well-manicured, and in the driveway sits a very nice, expensive car.

Without saying anything he gets out and strides around to my door. Pulling it open, he offers me his hand, and I take it, coming to a complete stand in front of him. He pushes the door shut behind me, then squeezes my hand and leads me to his front door. I wonder what he's thinking but get distracted. This guy is a bag of contradictions. Expensive clothes, flashy cars, the way he lets me—technically a stranger—take and use his credit card. But his home isn't as big or as fancy as I thought it would be. The door is an average white color with nothing special about it. Not even a fancy door knocker or bell.

When he steps inside, he flicks on a light. I'm not really sure what I expected to see when I walked in, but the fact that his home is plain really appeals to me. Sure it could do with a couple of personal touches. There isn't anything personal anywhere. But I like the simplicity of the black couches, television hanging on the wall, and a kitchen behind the main living room.

He throws the keys onto the kitchen island as he tugs me to the back glass door, which he slides open. Stepping outside, I notice a small pool with a few lounge chairs scattered around it and some fairy lights. He walks us to the edge of the pool, drops my hand, then presses a button that turns on a small water feature at the other end.

"I didn't bring my swimsuit," I tease.

"That's fine. You won't need one," he says, stepping back inside. I'm left standing outside in his landscaped garden. Once more, a contradiction to the impersonal interior. Outside holds a touch of warmth I find curious. A slight breeze rustles through the tall trees and fronds in the garden, adding a musical accompaniment to the nocturnal insects enjoying the garden as much as I am. Zuko reappears with a bottle of wine and two glasses.

"Are you being romantic right now?" I ask, brows raised. "You fuck me with a knife, and now it's all 'hey, let's have wine.'" He sits on one of the lounge chairs and pulls the other over so they're right next to each other, creating one large seat.

"Technically, I haven't fucked you tonight or this morning. So, no… Sit down and have a drink and see if it helps."

I roll my eyes as I sit next to him. After kicking off my shoes, I tuck my feet under my ass and take the glass he has poured for me.

"You haven't put drugs in here, have you?" I ask him before I take a sip.

"Why would you ask that and then proceed to drink it?" He's clearly baffled by my question and subsequent action.

"Hey, a girl has to sleep," I say, drinking the whole glass and giving it back to him. He takes and refills it as I lie back and stare at the sky.

"What are your nightmares about?"

"I never told you I had nightmares." I turn to look at him.

"You didn't have to," he replies gently.

"Tell me something about you I don't know, and I might tell you about me." I take the glass from his hand and glance back to the sky.

"I enjoy killing."

I blink, then blink again. *Did he?* Turning ever so slowly, I fix my gaze on his, unable to speak. "You know who I am. Do you really think the rumors aren't true?"

"I…" My pause causes him to raise an eyebrow and stare at me with disbelief in his eyes.

"You knew. You just didn't believe. Or didn't want to believe."

"What do you enjoy about it?" I ask him because I want to know why, why do any of us take the paths that are put in front of us. Me, working two jobs because I have a fear of running out of money, or the fact I can't stand to be touched, and then there is him.

I don't know what is more worrying. That I'm lying next to a man that just admitted he likes killing, or the fact that I'm not as bothered by it as I should be.

"It's not something a normal person would enjoy… I get it. But it's something I am good at. The best, even. And I'm relied upon heavily in this business. I am that last resort, the one people use when there is nowhere to turn. Well, myself and my brothers. If no one else can complete the hit, they hire us. And we always accomplish the task. There is no such thing as a failure rate for us."

"Should you be telling me this stuff? I mean…

it's not like you go around sharing with people what you do, right?"

"No, I don't talk to people *at all*. Unless it's my brothers."

"Must be nice to have that constant support," I add in a small voice.

"You have no family?" he asks.

"Nope, just me."

"Why are you having nightmares?"

"Just your everyday nightmares. Foster child shit. You know…going from home to home with no one really loving you."

"Lies," he says.

I huff out a sigh and decide if he can be honest with me, then I should do the same. "Okay fine. I watched one of my foster fathers beat my foster mother to within an inch of her life and then proceed to do the same with their son. That shit still fucks me up."

"Did he hurt you?" Zuko asks.

"I hid. He called out for me for what felt like hours, and I was terrified. I hid in the kitchen, watching the blood from his wife soak the floor. Her eyes were wide open, and blood ran in rivers everywhere."

"What happened to him?"

"When he didn't find me, he took a gun and shot himself in the head. Which, when you think about it, is selfish considering what he did to them." Glancing at Zuko, his eyes are firmly attached to mine.

"What?" I ask.

"I can see where you get your attitude from. Having to care for yourself your whole life..." He adds, "It either breaks us or makes us."

"And what did it do to you?"

"Oh, I'm all kinds of fucking broken. Not even God himself could put me back together." He winks.

Fuck.

He winked.

Panties, meet the floor.

"I think we're all a little broken. Some simply hide it better." I lift the glass to my lips and finish off the wine before I place it next to me. "The real question is...how do we put ourselves back together?"

"If you figure it out, don't let me know. I prefer myself the way I am."

I smile at his answer. *How many people do you meet that are as fucked-up as him and can be that honest?* Hell, actually, they all probably do, as they don't see anything wrong with themselves. I guess that's a better way to look at the way you are rather than trying to psychoanalyze yourself every day as to why you do certain things. I admire his honesty.

"I'm taking my car soon and going home," I announce.

"How have you been getting to work?" he asks.

"I either drive my old car, or Louise takes me."

He hands me the keys without another word and pulls me over to him.

SEVENTEEN

Zuko

SHE HAS a thing with people touching her but doesn't seem to mind when I do, and I like that the most. Somehow throughout the morning, she has worked her way over to my lounger and is between my legs, her head on my stomach, and her arms wrapped around me.

I pull the sunshade over her as I hear the glass door slide open. There are only ever two people who it could be—my brothers—no one else has access to or would dare step foot inside my home.

She moves a little, and her head nestles into my stomach as I spot Kenzo. He freezes, and Kyson comes up behind him with a big dirty smirk all over his face. My hand strokes her hair—lavender, such an odd color—but it suits her personality to a T.

"You brought her back?" Kyson asks as he bends down and looks at her sleeping on me.

For someone who hates to be touched, she sure is doing a lot of it.

"Why?" he adds, studying her. "I mean, there is a pool. Did you bring her here to drown her?" He meets my eyes, a devilish gleam in his.

I shake my head and give him a bored look. This is why you don't share things about your sex life with your brothers because they bring it up anytime and every-fucking- time they can.

"She's really pretty," Kenzo notes, taking the spare seat next to me, the one she was in before she decided after one to many wines to fall asleep on me.

"Too pretty to kill?" Kyson laughs, still standing above us.

"What are you doing here?" I ask them.

"Pops called. He wants to add more to our schedules." I bite my tongue at Kyson's words. *Of course he does.* "He's becoming greedy these days now that he has a little plaything," he adds.

"That's because she is spending all his money," Kenzo states. "She's the definition of a gold digger and not even a good one."

"He knows we aren't taking on more jobs than

necessary. We've played his game long enough," I declare.

Kyson scratches the back of his head. "Yeah, well… You better be telling him that because he seems to think otherwise."

I feel an almost imperceptible twitch and look down to find Alaska is now awake.

"Do you plan to say hello?" I ask. "Or lie there cuddling into me a little longer?" I question further with a grin.

She pulls back and sits up between my legs. "I was *not* cuddling you. You got me drunk and roofied my drink." She doesn't stand or make a move to the other lounger, just stays right where she is. Her eyes find my brothers, and she smiles up at them. "Your brother is an ass. Did you know that?" Kenzo blinks a few times with a nonchalant smirk, and Kyson smiles.

"Oh, we know, but it's interesting that you know so early."

She rolls her eyes and attempts to stand with a little stagger. "What's the time?" She doesn't reach for her bag while waiting for me to answer. "Time?" She taps her wrist, which is bare.

I glance at my watch and tell her, "Ten a.m."

Her eyes go wide. "I've been asleep *that* long?"

she questions as if she can't believe it. "Where have you been while I slept?"

I motion to where I am with my hand, and her brows raise. "You've stayed in that position the whole time? Are you crazy? Did you sleep?"

"No."

"He is crazy! As in the real kind. Just thought I would let you know so you're aware of that tidbit of info as well," Kyson interjects.

"You two are twins, aren't you?" she asks, pointing to them. "I mean… I see it with the dark hair and fuck-me eyes, but you don't look identical."

"We're fraternal twins," Kenzo explains.

"Hot," she says with an eye roll and then turns back to me. "I need to shower, pee, and go home." Squeezing between us, she reaches for her bag and throws it over her shoulder. "Thanks for the sleep or…whatever."

"We can cuddle any time," I yell as she makes her way to the door.

"That won't happen again," she shouts back over her shoulder before she disappears. I sit frozen, unable to move, until Kenzo punches me in the chest.

"Stop falling for the lunatic waitress."

"I like her," I add.

"Yeah, but you don't really like anyone."

I shrug my shoulders as I stand. When I'm fully upright, I see a wet patch on my pants.

"Did you come… or?" Kyson asks, noticing it as well.

"No, she drooled."

"Hmm…" is his noncommittal reply.

"Talk to Pops," Kenzo says, stripping off his shirt and jumping into the pool. Kenzo would jump into the pool even if it was frigid weather. It's chilly, but it's not too cold for a swim.

"He only listens to you."

"Yeah, yeah…" I wave them off and head to my bathroom. I pull my phone out of my pocket and I press call. It rings and rings, but she doesn't answer.

Seems I like two women.

One I fuck in real life.

The other I fuck over the phone.

When she doesn't pick up, I send her a message. It says it was delivered, so I can see she isn't ignoring me, not like she did when I sent her a picture of my hand. I was hoping she would give me something in return. Even a tiny piece of herself would be enough *for now*.

I want to know what she looks like.

I want to know who it is I've been talking to these last few months.

I had my brothers search for her number, but it's a burner phone, so no luck in that department. They said they might be able to track its location but not precisely, just when it pings on the towers. I've always said no, but I think it's time I started saying yes.

I *will* find her.

And I *will* meet her.

One thing I haven't shared with her is that when I hunt, I always catch my prey.

EIGHTEEN

Alaska

THE OTHER NIGHT I had the best night's sleep imaginable using Zuko as my pillow.

He's tried calling me, but not *me*. He's been calling Sage—the other *me*. He doesn't have my private number, and I'm not sure I want to tell him that we are the same person.

I like him not knowing.

I like that I have that part of him that he doesn't realize he is giving away.

Not that he gives away too much, but still, having that small part is pretty awesome.

Upon walking out of my apartment, I lock the door behind me. I'm going to the corner store, where I plan to buy chocolate ice cream—*a lot of it*

—and then return home to sit on the couch and watch horror movies and enjoy my night off.

"Alaska." I stop dead in my tracks, keys in hand, as *that voice* comes from beside me. "Do you plan to face me?"

"How did you find where I live?" I ask, turning to him. I hate that his features are highlighted under the moonlight and that he is so incredibly fucking sexy.

"I hunt, Alaska."

"Are you hunting me?"

"No, but I'm good at finding people."

"Okay then…" I trail off, dangling my keys in my hand, not really having any idea what to say to that.

"It's my brothers' birthday," he tells me. "They have a party happening right now. Would you care to attend?"

My mouth thins as I stare at him with my brows pulled together in confusion. It's a little last minute wouldn't you say? Your other date fall through?"

"Come to the party, Alaska."

"Why?"

"Because I invited you." He says those words like it should be obvious to me.

"What do I get out of it?"

"Where were you about to go?" he inquires, motioning to the keys in my hand.

I glance down at them and reply, "Ice cream."

"I'll buy you some on the way." He steps closer and reaches for my hand, pulling me to him, so our bodies crash into each other. "I'll buy you whatever the fuck you want if it means I get to fuck you again."

"Does it turn you on, buying me things?" I ask, feeling his taut body against mine.

"No, *you* turn me on. There's a big difference."

I reach down and slide my hands between us, so I can feel his cock. It bounces when I palm it and I can feel it's already semi-hard through his pants. I take a step back and drop my hand. He chuckles under his breath as he turns and moves toward his car.

"Just so you know, there are a bunch of strippers and whores at the party, so don't be surprised," he warns, opening the passenger door for me.

"So why are you here with me when you could be there fucking whoever the fuck you want?" I reach the car and grip the edge of the door, peering at him over the glass.

He reaches forward, touches my chin, and grips

it hard. "It's you I want to fuck. Haven't we established this fact already?"

I scoff, pull away, and get into his car.

Zuko shuts the door behind me, then strides around to the driver's side. When he's seated, he starts the car and says my name. I turn my head in his direction and watch as he undoes his belt and slides his hard cock out, then his hand grips it tight as he strokes. "See, all for you!" He growls out the words. His hips jerking as his breath rushes out his mouth.

A sly grin spreads over his face as he pulls out of the spot and heads to the party, his cock still out and standing tall.

What the actual fuck?

I can't stop staring.

It stays hard, and at some point, during the drive, I reach over and touch it.

"Are you sure you want to do that?" he asks, eyes remaining firmly on the road ahead of us. My hand squeezes around him. "Last time we fucked, I was gentle, but I can't promise that again."

"What do you plan to do to me?" I ask, placing my hand back in my lap.

We pull to a stop, and I pay attention to my surroundings for the first time since we got on the road. In front of me is a mansion with expensive cars parked everywhere. Women—some with no tops on—are dancing on the green, manicured lawn. The double front doors are wide open, and as I open my car door, I hear the heavy beat of loud music ring through my ears.

"I wonder if I will make you run again," Zuko muses.

"You'll only chase me," I reply over my shoulder.

He chuckles, and I love the sound of his deep rumble.

"Yes, I think I will."

I move forward, not caring that it's not my party and that I probably won't know a single person there. Walking past the two topless girls, I can't figure out if I'm overdressed or underdressed in my dark skinny jeans and black tee. I check over my shoulder to see if Zuko is watching them but he doesn't even glance their way because his eyes are firmly on my ass. I continue until I see one of his brothers—the more bubbly, talkative one—on the table, dancing with three women around him.

"I thought they were twins. Isn't this a party for both of them?" I ask Zuko as he comes up behind me.

"Kenzo doesn't like to party," he replies, placing his hand on my ass. I step away from his touch and head out back. There, I find his other brother sitting on the edge of the pool with an older man next to him. They both glance my way as Zuko comes to stand next to me.

"Happy birthday," I say to his brother.

"Who invited you?"

I flick my thumb to the side and point to Zuko.

He nods and throws out a "thanks" as the older man next to him studies me. He isn't old, but he is older than the three of them. Where Zuko appears to be in his mid-thirties, and the twins possibly late twenties or even early thirties, the other guy looks to be in his late forties, maybe even fifties, with salt and pepper hair and white beard. He stares at me as if I'm a threat, not a plaything. *Okay, that's a little odd. Who is this guy?*

I can't recall ever having a man stare at me like that before. I can't say I like it.

"This is Pops," Zuko says, nodding to the man.

Old Guy nods his greeting, and his attention is quickly diverted by a woman in an incredibly short red dress and bright-red heels stepping up behind him and tapping his shoulder.

"You better not be looking," she warns as she throws her hair over her shoulder.

Kenzo shakes his head and turns back to us.

I hear two girls giggle in the pool, and on closer inspection, they are naked. "Do you swim, Alaska?" Kenzo asks, and they all look at me.

"Sure."

Kenzo peels his shirt off, exposing a tattooed torso. Unlike his brother Kyson, who is clean, he's covered almost completely in ink. After removing his pants, he slides into the pool, and the two women start to giggle. "You have to be naked to enter this pool." He winks at me.

A girl steps out and grabs hold of Zuko's shoulder, leaning up and whispering something in his ear. He doesn't seem to really be listening as his eyes search mine before they flick to his brother. I shrug off my shirt and shimmy my jeans down in one smooth move, then kick off my shoes as I make my way toward the water. Stopping at the edge of the pool, I pull my underwear down my legs and leave them at the edge before I climb in. Turning around I lock eyes with Kenzo.

"Happy?" I ask.

"Yes, very much so."

Just as I'm getting used to the water, I feel a

hand wrap around my arm and tug me backward.
Zuko's narrowed eyes and red face stare back at me
in anger as he reaches for me and lifts me—as if I
weigh nothing—out of the pool. He instantly
removes his shirt and pulls it over my head,
Enveloping me in his heady scent. I go to speak, but
he lifts me up and throws me over his shoulder,
covering my ass with his hand as he stalks away.

"Bye, boys. It was nice meeting you, Pops, and
seeing you again, Kenzo," I yell out.

I hear Zuko groan as we enter the house. At
first, I think he's going to take me home, but
instead, he moves to the stairs.

"Where are you going?" Kyson asks. At least it
sounds like Kyson because I can't really tell since
I'm upside down and facing Zuko's back.

"Going to fuck some sense into her," Zuko grits
out as he grips my ass harder.

"Ha, good luck." *Yeah, it's definitely Kyson.* "Hi,
Alaska, don't die." Kyson chuckles, and I roll my
eyes as Zuko heads up the stairs. We enter a dark-
ened room, and I can hardly see anything, but when
he puts me down, I know it's a bed under me.

As soon as his hands are empty, he reaches for
his shirt that I am wearing and pulls it off over my
head, before discarding it. I can just make out his

shape as I hear him remove his pants and drop them to the floor. I crawl to the edge of the mattress and reach up to touch him.

"Do you have any kinks?" he asks, his hand finding my breast, massaging it before he squeezes the nipple and continues his journey down my body.

"Me? Um… I like to come."

"Yes, that's something I have helped you achieve already." His voice sounds smug and somewhat condescending, but all it does is make me smirk.

"Yes. So if you could do that again…" I trail off as his hand stops on my pussy.

"You shouldn't have shown them." The words growled, and there's a tone that demands attention.

"Shown them what?"

"Your body."

"Why? Afraid they will like what they see?" I taunt.

"Afraid I'll have to kill my brother if he mentions what he saw. Or Pops. You can do what you want, but I'd prefer not to kill my family."

"So, you're saying if I got naked in another pool, you would be okay with that as long as your family isn't there?" I sass.

He smacks my pussy, and I yelp. He pulls me

back to him, leans down, and kisses my cheek. "That would be fine. I'd happily kill them."

I can't help but huff out a soft laugh at his words.

"I have a kink," he states. "It involves your breathing."

His mouth is now in front of mine, and I can feel his breath tickle my face. I've heard of breath play, which usually involves choking, and I'm down for a bit of choking if it gets me off. I hear the crinkle of a wrapper as one hand works sliding it on.

I move my hand down until I reach his hard cock. *Fuck, has it been hard since the moment we got in the car?* I lift myself up and grip his shoulders before I wrap my legs around him, and he holds me still so we don't fall.

"You can play with me, just *no* knives."

"Are you sure?" he asks. "No running this time."

"No running," I confirm as I take him inside me.

Zuko grunts as he enters me but lets me do all the work. I slide myself up and down his length over and over, up and down, until he takes over, picking up the pace.

I like giving into his power.

What he does to me.

Zuko lays me back on the bed, and my hands find the sheets, clutching them tight. He holds on to my hips and switches things up. He begins to thrust in and out ever so slowly, torturing me with pleasure. My muscles tense with rapture and I'm lost in him. He pulls out, grips my waist, and flips me over. I moan at the loss of his fullness, but he pulls my ass back so it's in the air before he grabs a handful of my hair and yanks my head off the mattress. I moan as his cock rubs along the outside of my pussy but doesn't slide back in. Then I hear a crinkling noise, but it's not the same sound as a condom wrapper.

"No running, and don't freak out," he says.

"Okay," I whisper. And before I even know what's happening, something is pulled over my head and then gripped around my neck as he slides straight into me. I drop to my elbows, my hands reaching for what's covering my face and tearing at it.

He pumps in and out, one hand holding whatever it is and the other reaching between me and playing with my clit. He fucks me while I struggle to breathe, my fingers fumbling at what seems to be plastic.

And then I'm groaning as I come.

How the hell did I just come?

I feel it all over my body, but I can hardly breathe.

Oh. My. God.

Just as I start to freak the fuck out, whatever is on my face and neck is lifted away, and I'm flipped over as something warm touches my clit. His mouth is now on me, tasting and licking me in extremely slow movements. His finger slips inside, and in a few strokes, I come even harder than I could possibly imagine.

What was that?

How was that?

I can't…

A light flicks on, and I find him smirking as he gazes down at me, his cock still semi-hard, appearing like it could go another round.

Next to me is a plastic bag.

I grind my teeth as I glare at him for fucking me with a plastic bag over my damn head.

What the actual fuck!

NINETEEN

Zuko

SHE JUMPS up from the bed and, in one swift movement, slaps my face.

Hard.

I let her.

I mean, I didn't expect her to like it, but she loved it.

The problem now is that she can't admit it without feeling like she has a kink.

"*You tried to suffocate me!*" she screams, grabbing the bag and trying to put it over my head. I pull it away from her, and her eyes search around for something to wear. When she only sees my shirt, she scoops it up and slides it on. "Take me home, or I'll fucking walk. I don't care either way," she barks, heading to the door.

"You came though, right?" I ask from behind her as I struggle to pull on my pants quickly and follow behind her, but she's already down the stairs and in the living room. She's stopped by Pop's play-thing, and they exchange a few words.

Alaska's furious eyes meet mine as she marches out the front door.

"Shit, what have you done now?" Kyson asks, coming up next to me. I ignore him and follow Alaska, only to see her trying to break into my car. I click the key fob, and she pulls the door open with an almighty yank and gets in, slamming the door behind her.

Climbing into the car next to her, she has turned so her body is facing the door. I can hear her teeth grinding, so I can only imagine the death glare she would be giving me right now.

"I did warn you," I state matter-of-factly.

"And I didn't run. Did I?" she bites back, still not looking at me.

I start the car and drive away from the party. "Alaska."

"I despise you," she says, but her voice shakes. "You and your fucked-up sex. First, it was a knife, and now it's a fucking plastic bag. I mean…" she takes a deep stuttering breath, "if you thought I was ugly and you couldn't stand to look at my face, tell me, don't fucking suffocate me."

"I warned you," I tell her again and hit the steering wheel with my palms. "And you are anything but ugly. You're fucking divine." I hope she can hear the truth in my words. Never should that thought be in her head. She is anything but ugly.

"Yeah, yeah… I bet you say that to *all* the girls you fuck." I peer over at her and watch her shoulders rise and fall with her heavy breathing. Then, all of a sudden, she turns to face me. Her eyes show a mixture of everything I don't want to see written in them. "It all makes sense. The girl you tried to drown…" She sighs heavily. "Fuck. *Fuck!*" she yells as her place comes into view.

She reaches for her keys, which she left in the cupholder, and before I can even stop the car, she jumps out, turns around, and pins me with her stormy glare. "If I see you again, I *will* burn your fucking house down. You hear me?" She waits for me to reply, but when I don't, she slams the car door and runs to her front door. She struggles to open it, her hand is shaking that much, and she doesn't look back as she storms inside.

I smile at her anger, and for some reason, it turns me on.

But, fuck!

Did I fuck it up for good this time? I hope not.

It takes everything in me not to go and knock on her door and make her come out again. She will realize soon enough. That despite the fact that she is currently hating me, I know she had just as much fun as I did.

I head back home, taking the long route in hopes that when I get back my families curiosity will have dies down and I can avoid the inevitable questions. The minute I walk in the door I know I'm shit outta luck.

"You kill your date?" Pops asks.

I move past him and head to the refrigerator and grab a bottle of water.

"Why did she run?" Kyson questions as the music pumps through the house. He grabs a bottle of whiskey, keeping it for himself. The reason I don't drink is because Kyson loves to bury his demons with alcohol. Some of those demons which we are unaware of, I am not sure we will ever know the extent of his issues.

Kenzo will join Kyson on occasion, but he doesn't drink nearly as much as him.

"He probably tried to suffocate her," Kenzo pronounces as he enters the room. "Nice rack she has," he adds.

It takes two heartbeats before I am standing in front of him, my hand around his throat, holding him up off the floor. He struggles but doesn't fight me.

"Remove those images from your head," I demand.

He scratches at my hands, and finally I lower him back down. He bends over, hands on his knees and inhales gulps of air.

"Fuck, Z, she's a pussy with great tits. Why the fuck are you so worked up? Aren't you in love with whoever it is you call every fucking night," Kyson says, defending his twin.

Kyson saw her tits too? He wasn't out there. Fucker must've saw her tits through the glass door. I spin around to face him, and he holds up his hands. "Calm the fuck down."

"Didn't you just get laid? Why are you so mad?" Kenzo huffs.

I turn to see Pops watching us. He's used to us fighting, but the slight smirk on his lips has me thinking he's onto me.

"None of your business," I tell them as I walk

over to the music and turn it off. The few people who are left glance my way, and I wave to the door. "Everyone…*fucking*…leave."

Pops checks around—it is his house, after all. He nods and pours himself a whiskey. I open my bottle of water and nearly down the whole thing in one go. I guess now is as good as ever to talk to Pops.

Kyson eyes me and as if he can read my mind shakes his head, indicating he doesn't want me to talk to him. Maybe now isn't the time.

Fine with me.

I can wait.

For now.

She is teaching me to be a patient man.

And now I have to tell Sage…

TWENTY

Alaska

"YOU'VE REACHED Sage from You Beat It, We Spit It. First, let's start with your name." I answer the phone as I pop a piece of popcorn in my mouth and sit on my couch. I took the week off work at the bar, not because I wanted to, but because I have been sick. Stupid flu. Though, I probably needed the time off anyway to regroup and recover.

"Sage…"

I know that voice straight away—it's easy for me to recognize being around it so much. I'm sure I could pick it out in a crowd, no matter what. Shivers rack my body when he speaks again. "I've missed you."

"Have you, though?"

"I have," he replies.

"You do know when you call now that you only ask me questions. You don't call to listen to me anymore," I state.

"That's because I get enjoyment from your company. All your company." After a moment, he adds, "You sound off."

"I am off. I'm eating popcorn and watching horror movies. It's really putting me off."

"Of what?"

"Men," I reply, smiling to myself.

"I hope not this one."

My smile drops.

I hate that I like hearing his voice.

I hate it a lot.

This man tried to suffocate me.

Fuck me to death.

I mean, come on?

My childhood really messed me up.

"I called to tell you this will be the last time we talk."

"Why?"

"It's not you I want."

My mouth opens in shock. *What?*

"I told you before that I met someone."

"Yes, I remember."

"Well, I'm at her door right now, and I hope to

God she will let me in." My heart rate picks up. Getting up off the couch, I drop the popcorn on the floor and almost drop my phone too. "But I had to tell you first. I had to tell you this is it."

"Okay…"

"Goodnight, Sage."

And then the line goes dead, and a knock sounds on my door. I freeze, thinking if I stay quiet he'll go away, but then he knocks again. And again.

"Your lights are on, Alaska, and I can see you standing there."

Right, of course, if I can see the outline of his head through the door, it means he can see me too.

"Fuck off," I shout.

"Come out and speak to me."

"No."

"You can't still be mad."

"Oh, I'm fucking livid," I yell. "I warned you what would happen if I saw you again."

"Technically, you can't see me, just the outline," he says, being a smartass. "So no burning anything," he adds.

"You can leave now." I walk back to my couch and sit down.

"Alaska." He says my name again, and it only makes me angrier. I pick up my glass and throw it at the door. It smashes all over my tile floor, and I cuss because it's me who is going to have to clean that up when technically, it's his fault for being an ass.

He's such a fuckhead.

With a great cock.

And a great mouth.

***

The following week I go back to work, and Louise is ecstatic to see me. She gives me one of her famous hugs and doesn't let go until I push her away.

"Did the soup help?" she asks. Louise popped around a few times and brought me soup every time. I've never really had a friend like her, and I appreciate her a lot. Enough to even put up with her hugs, but only until it's too much for me to handle.

Apart from Zuko's unwelcome visit, she is the only person who came by while I was sick.

"Yes, it did. Thank you." I pull out my work shirt and exchange it for the top I have on.

"So, word on the street is that the Hunter brothers come here regularly now," she mentions.

"Huh?" I don't know what she's talking about at

first, but then I remember. "Oh, that's right, you know them."

"I don't really know them, per se. We just come from the same neighborhood," she replies. "But they don't go out as much as they have been, and word is out that Zuko has a lady." I freeze at her words, and then she surprises me when she adds, "You."

I turn to face her. "Me?"

"Yes, you were at a party with him. Naked, from what I hear. It's the buzz everywhere. Considering those men are never seen in public with anyone unless they are fucking them it's got everyone talking."

"That's all we did. We fucked."

"Yes, I gathered that much from him carrying you around naked and all."

"You heard that too?" I ask, slightly embarrassed.

"Yes. From what I hear, and I quote, 'He is protective over you.'" She puts her quote fingers down and shrugs. "Anyway, you are the talk of the town, and it's been said to stay away from you now that you are Zuko's girl."

"I am *no one's girl*," I snap, quickly finishing getting dressed. *I want to punch him in the face.* "If someone says I am, set them straight." She nods but smiles as she does so.

"For what it's worth, I think he's met his match with you."

"I'm not seeing him again."

"Too late, he's here," she informs me, and I stop mid-step, halting before I get to the door.

Spinning around, I lock eyes with her. "Are you joking?"

"Nope. And his table has requested you."

"That's it. I'm quitting." I throw my hands up as I stomp back to my locker.

"No, don't let a man win. You are a boss-ass bitch, and one day I hope to be like you." Her hands land on my shoulders, and she squeezes.

Ha! Never heard anyone in my life say they want to be like me. I'm what mothers are afraid their daughters will turn into.

"You take his table," I tell her. "I'll take yours." She bites her lip as if she's unsure. "If they don't tip you, you can have half of what I make."

"Okay, but remember what happened last time. He didn't want me to serve him." She shrugs and walks out with me. I don't look in the direction of his table. It's best I don't. It's not like I can get him kicked out of here. After all, he has connections that I'm not even aware of. I found that out when he had Sarah fired.

Jeff is behind the bar when we approach, which is not like him. But tonight is busy, and they could use the extra hands. He scowls when he lays eyes on me and goes back to pouring whatever drink he is mixing.

Louise leans over and yells in my ear, "What do I say if he asks for you? His brothers are with him tonight. And two others…a girl and an older man."

"Tell them I'm already booked." That's all I can come up with as I grab the tray and make my way to the opposite side of the bar to start my night. An hour goes by in a flash. I'm serving a bunch of girls celebrating their twenty-first with their rich daddy, who, I might add, tips extremely well. I do prefer serving the women, but the men tip a shitload better.

And it does help he can't seem to keep his eyes off me.

Walking back to the bar and not once glancing in Zuko's direction, I pay no attention until a hand lands on my hip. I turn, smiling, thinking it's a regular customer, until I see Zuko's face.

"Are you ignoring me, Trouble?"

"I told you I *never* want to see you again. I'm

pretty sure I didn't stutter when I said it." I pull away from him, and his hand drops from my hip while I take a moment to drink him in. He's dressed in black jeans and a button-up black shirt. A nice, shiny watch glints on his wrist.

Zuko is handsome, but just because someone is good-looking and can make you come, it doesn't mean you should give them everything.

Respect is earned.

Not given.

"What can I do to change your mind?"

I shake my head and turn to leave. Just as I feel he is about to follow me, I swing around and hold up my hand. "Listen…is it that hard for you to comprehend?" I almost scream at him.

Jeff walks by and halts when he catches us arguing. He steps over, and I take a step back, putting more room between Zuko and myself.

Zuko stares at me as Jeff speaks. "Is there a problem?" I'm not sure if he's asking Zuko or me.

"Was it the bag that pushed it over the edge?" Zuko asks with absolutely no shame and no fricking filter, like I want the world to know what happened between us. "Because if I remember correctly, your mind may have hated it, but your body certainly did not."

Fuck him. I spin and head straight to the bar, leaving him standing there with Jeff. I glance over my shoulder and note that Jeff is talking to Zuko. Zuko half-ass pays attention before his gaze finds me again. I glare at him for a beat, and then I turn my back on him.

"So, the old man is doing all the ordering, and the rest aren't doing a thing. Zuko has asked me twice when his regular server will be back," Louise says, coming up next to me.

"Tell him to suffocate himself," I grumble, then add, "Those exact words. Trust me."

"Um…"

I grab her arm and squeeze. "Those *exact* words. Tell him they're from me."

She gives me a baffled look as her brows pinch together and her lips thin but heads back to Zuko's table, where he is now sitting with his brothers and two other people I can't make out from here. Louise leans down and speaks to him. It's hard to tell what exactly he says or does back, but his eyes find mine straight away. And when they do, a shiver breaks free over my body.

Quickly looking away, I accidentally run into someone in my haste to get away. Before I can apologize, I feel something sharp stab me in the belly, which is an odd sensation. I look up, only to see Sarah standing there, a hoodie covering her head and a knife in her damn hand.

She leans in close as she whispers in my ear, "Payback is a bitch." I go to reach for her hoodie to pull her back, but a sharp pain runs through me allowing Sarah to get away. Placing my hand over my stomach where it hurts, I feel a warm wet sensation. When I lift my hand away from the wound my fingers are sticky with my own blood.

Fuck, that hurts.

Bending over and falling down clutching my stomach, I try to think of the best way to get off this fucking floor with no one hurting me even more. I have a high pain tolerance.

But this…

This hurts like a bitch.

"He didn't say anything back to me, but he did look at me like he wanted to kill me," Louise chirps when she reaches my side. She doesn't notice that something's wrong.

I'm still bent over, not able to move.

"What's the deal with the bag? When I said that, his eyes went wide for a second," she rambles. "Alaska, can you hear me?" I can, but I can't say anything back. Her hand lands gently on my back.

"Do you have period pains? Is it that time of the month?" She rubs my back as I grip the bar's edge and hold on for dear life. "Fuck, Alaska, there is blood on the floor." Her hand leaves my back, and she moves in front of me, then drops down into a crouch so she can see me better.

"Oh my gosh you're bleeding?"

I groan and squeeze my eyes shut.

Talking hurts.

I don't want to talk.

"*Alaska*... Why is there blood coming from your hand?" Her hand lifts to touch mine on my stomach, but I basically growl at her. "Did you cut yourself?"

No, I absolutely did not.

But again, the words don't leave my mouth.

"I'll be back." And then she's gone, and I wonder once more how the hell I am going to move without hurting myself more. *And how did I let that bitch stab me? How?*

Small specs of light dance around my eyes and nausea washes over me.

"Alaska..."

I hate that voice as much as I love that voice.

"I'm going to pick you up now. Don't move your hand." All I can do is nod my agreement. And when I do, one of Zuko's arms wraps around the backs of my legs while the other slides around my back as he gently lifts me. I stay in my bent position, unable to move.

Fuck. Everything hurts.

And then everything goes black.

TWENTY-ONE

Zuko

HER HAND DROPS from her stomach, and I can see the blood straight away. Louise, who came and got me straight away is next to her, quickly places her hand over the wound as I hurry her out.

"Will she be okay?" Louise asks.

My car is already out front, so I quickly lay her in the backseat. Louise stands behind me, her hand now covered in blood, looking worriedly at Alaska.

"I'll take care of her. Give me your phone." She hands it to me, and I quickly input my number and call my own phone. "I'll call you with an update. Go back to work." I shut the door and speed off. A soft groan comes from Alaska, but she doesn't wake.

I drive down back alleys until I reach Mr. Rennes's house. He's a doctor for the underground.

He's expensive, but his discretion is always on point, and he has dealt with these types of situations before.

And to be honest, the hospital is the last place I think of when I need something fixed.

As soon I pull up to his apartment building, I reach for Alaska, and she opens her eyes. Those almost lavender-colored eyes find mine before they close again. Her white blouse is covered in blood.

I didn't see what happened or who did this to her.

But believe me, I *will* find the who.

Kicking Mr. Rennes's door with my foot, I hear rustling from the other side before it opens. A salt-and-pepper-haired man stands on the threshold staring back at me, dressed in only a red robe and glasses as big as his eye sockets.

"Mr. Hunter, it's not every day I get the pleasure of seeing you." He steps back and waves me in. He's right. I can stitch myself up, and rarely do I need to come and see the good old doctor. My brothers, on the other hand, prefer the drugs the doctor offers when he needs to fix them up.

"Who is she?" he asks as I step into the back room.

"Mine."

He sweeps everything off the counter and motions for me to put her down. He quickly slides on a pair of gloves before he touches her.

"Looks to be a stab wound. Isn't that deep and luckily hasn't hit anything major," he says and waves for me to step back. I don't, and he lets out a heavy sigh as he goes to work around me.

I touch her hair, brushing it back as she lies there. "Why isn't she awake?" I ask.

"Probably passed out from the pain," he replies. "I'm sure she will wake soon." He numbs the area before he starts cleaning and stitching the wound. With every stitch he makes I feel my blood boil that much hotter. When he's on the last stitch, her eyes flutter open.

At first I see confusion, then fear, then utter panic and she goes to scramble backward on the table, but I hold her down as the doctor finishes.

"Stay still," I order softly. "It's almost over."

"What are you doing?" She gasps.

"Fixing you," the doctor answers, giving her a smile. "All done, love. I would suggest some pain medication, as it's going to hurt when the numbing wears off."

Alaska looks at him, then me, and her eyes close for a second before they reopen.

"I need to sit up."

"Carefully," the doctor cautions.

With quick steps, I move around to the side and offer her my hand. When she has hold of it, I slowly pull her up.

She groans and shakes her head. "That crazy bitch," she hisses.

"Who?" I ask.

Her eyes narrow. "It's your fault, you know?"

I smirk at her, not knowing what she is implying. "Don't you look at me like that," she bites out.

"Like what?"

"Like you want to fuck me again."

"There isn't a moment that goes by that I don't want to fuck you. But who is the bitch?"

"Sarah, the one you got fired. Guess now it's me who pays the price for your fuckups." She attempts to get off the table, and I help her, but as soon as one foot hits the floor, she sways on her feet and groans again. I pick her up, careful not to hurt her.

"I'll handle it," I declare.

"No, you *will not*," she says as forcefully as she can manage. "I know what you do."

"Yes, don't we all. Here, take these, please." The doctor hands her some pills and explains when to take them. She thanks him, and when we get out to the car, I place her in the backseat and reach for the bag in the front before I return to the doc.

Passing him his payment, he looks past me to her.

"You like her. It's good for you," he states.

"I don't come here for advice," I tell him, giving him extra money for his trouble.

"I know, you never needed it. But in case you do, I'm here." He nods and steps back. I shake my head as I walk back to the car. Peering in the back, Alaska's head is leaning against the window on the opposite side of the car.

"Your place or mine? And word to the wise, whichever location you choose, I'm not leaving you tonight. Doctor's orders."

Her eyes narrow at me before she speaks. "Yours."

TWENTY-TWO

Alaska

"WHO WAS THAT?" I finally ask. I've been quiet for most of the car ride here. Contemplating how I can get out of this situation.

"He's a doctor."

"Why didn't you take me to the hospital?"

"Do you want to report the stabbing? Because they would have made you." I absorb his words. "Or would you rather *I* deal with it?"

"You deal with it?" I ask, confused.

"Yes, I can deal with it."

"How?"

He pulls up to his house. "Any which way you please."

"What if I asked you to leave it alone?"

He gets out of the car, comes around to my side,

then opens the car door and stares down at me. "You don't want her to suffer after what she's done to you?"

"Do you?" I take his offered hand and wince when I stand, my hand instantly going to my stomach.

"Yes, very much so." His jaw is set, and his brows are furrowed.

"It's not you who was stabbed."

"I've been stabbed before," he says.

"What did you do to that person?"

"Well, the first time, I gave him a black eye…" He smirks. "It was Kyson." My brows shoot up at that bit of information. "The second… I killed." He shrugs like it's nothing. "He obviously was not my brother and did not get a pass."

I pause in the doorway.

"I'm not sleeping with you," I declare.

"I'll take the couch." He nods to the house for me to enter. When we're both safely inside he locks the door. I like his house, even though it's so minimalist. I know he spends a lot of time here. It smells like him, and despite my wanting to hate that as well, it somehow comforts me.

"I'm only staying tonight," I warn.

"No, you will stay a minimum of two nights. I

need to change the dressing." I clench my jaw, but he ignores it and opens the door to his bedroom. "The sheets are fresh, and I'll get you something to sleep in." He opens a drawer and pulls out a black shirt, then passes it to me. "I can go and buy you fresh underwear if you prefer."

"I'll wear yours." He nods again, a smile teasing his lips as if he's happy with that answer and comes back holding a black pair of briefs. "You can leave now. I need to change." I nod to the door.

"And how do you expect to lift that tight shirt over your head?" he asks, eyeing the piece of clothing in question.

I turn around and give him my back. "Cut it off of me," I order. "It's not like I plan to wear it ever again."

His phone starts ringing loudly, and he takes it out of his pocket and places it on speaker before throwing it on his bed. "What?"

"Is she okay?" I hear the voice and know who it is straight away.

"Hey, Louise," I answer.

"Oh God, I feel so stupid. I was talking to you, and you were stabbed, and it didn't even register, Alaska. Shit, are you okay?"

"How did you get this number?" I ask, but she doesn't answer, Zuko does.

"I gave it to her so she can check on you." Something inside of me swells at the thought. I've never really had anyone care for me before. No one to look after me the way Zuko is. My appendix burst once, and they asked me who to put as my next of kin. I had no one. Now, I have two people. Both are forced, *I think*—one I plan to set his house on fire, and the other gives unwanted cuddles.

"Do you need anything? I can see you tomorrow," she offers.

"I need everything, and he won't let me go home," I complain as I hear a ripping sound. Zuko tears my shirt in half up my back and then moves around to face me as he removes the remnants of my shirt until I'm left standing in front of him in my bra.

"Okay, well, I'll call back in the morning to see what you want me to get for you. Get some rest. And I'm glad you are doing okay." She doesn't hang up after she speaks. I wait and glance at the phone, and after a few silent moments, she finally mumbles, "Who did it?"

"I'll tell you tomorrow," I reply.

Zuko reaches for the phone and hangs up on her before he comes to stand in front of me. "Sit."

I glance at his bed and do as he says.

He gets down on his knees and pulls off my boots one by one, followed by my socks. Standing, he places them at the door and comes back to me. "Sleep with the bra on or off?"

I reach for the clip, which just so happens to be at the front, and undo it. My tits fall free, but I don't care. Zuko's eyes lock on my chest before he reaches for his shirt and starts dressing me.

"Have you ever cared for anyone in your life?" I ask, just as he slides my arm through one of the holes carefully. He does the same with the other arm, not answering me until he pulls the sheets back on the bed.

"No." He motions for me to crawl in, but I don't move. "Am I doing okay?" he asks, unsure, and my heart skips a beat at his vulnerability. It's the first sign of this type of emotion that I have seen from him.

I'm far from the sappiest person. I have an exterior shell that is almost impossible to crack.

"We shall see." I grin as I lie back.

He leaves the room for a few minutes, then comes back with a glass of water and the pain medication the doc gave me and places it on the nightstand My eyes become heavy, but they follow him as he walks out and shuts the door behind him, taking my dirty clothes with him.

———

I wake up in pain.

In agony.

Every time I attempt to move, a bolt of torture shoots through me. Tears prick my eyes, and I don't know where my phone is to call Zuko. Actually, I don't even know if anyone grabbed it. Sighing, my head falls deeper into the pillow. I want to lie on my side. My body tries to go that way, with or without my consent, and sweat dots my forehead. I lie still for a while knowing it wasn't the pain that woke me and then it all comes flooding back. the

Stupid fucking nightmares.

The door opens slightly, and when I turn my head, Zuko is standing there.

"You screamed," he says. *Huh, I thought I did that in my head.* "Figured it was a nightmare," he adds.

"It was." I move wrong and yelp at the pain. He is at my bedside in three long strides. Scooping up the pills and holding the glass of water out to me.

"Painkillers. Take them."

I shake my head. "I usually don't sleep with painkillers but those look like they can knock a bear out. I don't want to go back to sleep."

"Scared of the nightmares?"

I pick at the imaginary lint on the covers.

"I…" He rounds the bed and sits on it. He doesn't get under the blanket next to me. Instead, he stays on top of it and turns to face me.

"What do you need?" he asks quietly.

"I don't know." He reaches out and touches my arm. tickling the skin softly as he strokes his fingers up and down. The feel of him doing that makes me smile.

"Why won't you let me deal with her?" he asks. I turn my head to face him, not moving any other part of my body. His hand maintains its gentle strokes, which are oddly comforting.

What is he doing? I feel my body relax. Or perhaps it's the pain medication. *Who knows.*

"Because you don't get that right," I reply.

"What do you plan to do to her?"

I turn back and stare up at the ceiling. "Maybe I should stab her too. See how she likes it," I mumble. "Or maybe I will just beat the living fucking shit out of her."

"I think both options are great," he says, with a hint of laughter in his voice. "Though I personally would go with the first." I turn to him and see a small smirk gracing his lips.

"You and your stupid knife."

"Your pussy says otherwise."

"I am still gonna burn your house down, you know. You didn't listen to me."

"Aren't you glad I didn't? Where would you be now?" he playfully fires back.

"In a hospital." I cover my mouth as I yawn.

"Yeah, but they wouldn't be able to help with your nightmares and lack of sleep."

"I'm sure there are drugs for that now," I say, knowing full well l wouldn't take them.

"Yeah, there probably are." He runs a fingertip over my cheek before saying my name. "Alaska…"

"Hmm…"

"I don't plan to let you go."

"I'm not yours to keep," I remind him.

"I know that, but you could be."

"Could you survive off not almost killing me every time you want to fuck?" I ask him seriously.

"Yes." His answer is immediate, and in some ways, that shocks me.

"I doubt that very much." My eyes start to become heavier and heavier.

"I would, for you. But the thing is…you can't accept how much you actually like it."

I don't respond to that.

Because my eyes close and I'm out.

TWENTY-THREE

Zuko

"IS SHE AWAKE?" Louise asks from the opposite side of my front door.

I don't invite her in because, frankly, I hate anyone coming into my home.

"Can I see her?" she asks, pushing her point.

"Yes, she can come in." I hear Alaska yell out from the bedroom.

Louise smiles and steps in, carrying a backpack with her. When she walks into my house and guides herself straight to my room, I almost lose my shit. That is until I spot Alaska, who has a soft smile on her face for Louise.

I was never sure if they were friends or not— they always seemed a bit off. Or maybe it was just

Alaska. Louise strolls in and sits next to Alaska on the bed and almost bounces as she does.

"I took your house keys from your locker and got you a few things," Louise tells her.

"Thanks, I need to shower. I can feel the dried blood on my body and it's pulling at my skin." She attempts to sit up, and I'm at her side in an instant and reaching for her. She waves me away, but I grab the spare pillow and stuff it behind her back.

"The hospital let you go home already?" Louise asks.

"Yeah, under supervision," Alaska lies. *Smart girl.*

"Who did it? Do you know?" she whispers to Alaska.

"Nope. It was dark, and I just remember feeling a sharp pain."

"Oh God, what if they do it to someone else next?" Louise frets.

"I've got the surveillance videos. I'll find the person before they do," I tell Louise, and she looks up at me.

"Okay, that makes me feel safer. Thank you."

Alaska rolls her eyes and goes to get off the bed. Louise stands, pulls the blankets down, and offers her a hand. Alaska takes it and puts her feet on the floor.

"Does it hurt much?" Louise whispers.

"Yes, *a lot*." Alaska winces.

I step out to grab a waterproof dressing to cover her wound so she can shower. When I return, she's already standing with her hand on Louise's shoulder. I nod to the shirt she's wearing, which is mine, and have to remind my cock not to get hard. Which it seems is always hard around her.

It's making lying next to her in bed difficult, but not so difficult that I'll interfere with her sleep.

Last night she fell asleep easily.

Even after she started softly snoring, I didn't stop moving my hand on her arm. And today, my arm feels like lead, but it worked. And she slept, which was what she needed.

"I need to change the dressing," I tell her.

"Okay, blood makes me sick, so I'm going to step out." Louise points to the door as I drop to my knees. Alaska lifts the shirt and checks her body. She's wearing my underwear and nothing else. Her skin still has some dried blood which is probably why she is complaining. I reach for her bandage, and she pulls back as I touch her.

"When I was a kid, it was my job to look after my brothers, not in the way you may think, in the way where if someone fucked with them, I would fuck with them." Her eyes find mine, and I glance back to her stomach and start carefully removing the bandage. She flinches but doesn't pull away this time. "As you can imagine, they were assholes. I mean… I guess I was too." I pause as I open the new bandage. She's watching me, waiting for more. "I even stabbed one of them once for pissing me off." I smile at the thought.

"Why are you smiling about hurting your brother?"

"Trust me when I say that bastard deserved it at the time." I chuckle.

"Why?"

"He threw a rock at my toe, and not just a small rock but one that took two hands to pick up. He crushed my toe. I got angry, and marched up to him, grabbed my knife, and stabbed him. He never took his anger out on me again. Kenzo never has, but Kyson's always been a bit wild."

"Your parents?" she asks.

"Non-existent. I mean, don't get me wrong, they were there. Until they weren't. I never cared for them anyway."

"Are they dead?"

"As far as I know." I haven't looked into it, and I couldn't care less. Just because you bring someone into this world, it doesn't give you any right to them, especially if you do a shit job at caring for them. "Have you ever thought about looking for your real parents?" I ask.

"Nope. I don't intend to either. I guess we're similar that way." I stand and step back. Her shirt falls back down, covering her body. "I need to shower." I give her my hand, and she takes it without fighting me. I walk her to the shower, then reach in and turn on the faucet. I spin back as she pulls her hand away and attempts to remove her shirt, but she winces as she lifts her arms to pull it off.

"Let me," I offer.

"I'm not having sex with you," she blurts. I fight the smirk touching my lips at her outburst. "I can see you. You know that, right?"

I tear the shirt instead of trying to lift her arms.

She laughs and shakes her head. "We could have gotten that off without tearing it."

"I'm rich. I can afford another one," I tell her, then motion to my underwear she is still wearing.

"I can get that." She pulls them down, stepping out of them before she treads into the shower. She doesn't care that she's naked in front of me now. "Did you sleep last night?" she asks as I lean against the wall, watching her. She grabs the soap and starts lathering it up over her body.

"I didn't."

"Why?" she asks.

"Because every time I attempted to stop touching you, you would twitch." Her hands pause their washing, and she locks eyes with me. "And if I fell asleep, I could have rolled over and hurt you."

"You never cared about hurting me before," she points out.

"That was different. I wasn't trying to hurt you. I was trying to please you, which, if you have forgotten, I did… *Twice*. Actually, you came more times than that."

Those eyes that set my fucking heart alight turn away from me.

I take a moment to scan her perfect body.

"You make me angry. You…just you and all that you are," she says. "We could never work. Not because I think you are fucking crazy, but because I am too. And two people equally as crazy as each other simply won't work. It would be a disaster. I need a man who calms me, not one who tries to strangle me." She steps out of the shower, and I hold the soft towel out to her. "And I would never ask you not to be who you are because that's only asking for trouble in the long run. So why even attempt to commit now when we both know how it will end?"

"You don't know how it will end," I argue. "And I didn't ask you to marry me. I want to fuck you and fuck you a lot."

She laughs and shakes her head as she steps closer to me. I'm careful not to touch her or to hurt her.

"I see good in you, even knowing who you are and what you do. Tell me, Zuko, does the hunter love the hunt?"

"I do. Very much so," I answer truthfully.

"And I want a normal life. As normal as I can get, that is."

"No such thing. Only fools believe in that." I open the bathroom door and see Louise sitting on the bed, waiting for us.

"Your house is boring," she states matter-of-factly, making Alaska laugh and then grunt in pain.

"Shit, don't make me laugh. That hurt," Alaska wheezes.

"What's wrong with my place?" I ask.

"It's boring. You have barely anything here. And we know you have money because Alaska here spent it. Maybe you should have asked her to spend some of it on things for your house."

"It's very…" Alaska pauses to think of the right word as she sits on the bed, "Zuko," she finally finishes, smiling.

"What's that supposed to mean?" I ask.

"It's just…you aren't flashy. You always dress in black. There's never any color. Nothing you wear is flashy, yet we both know you have the money like Louise said."

"I don't need material things. That's what gets people killed. I should know."

Louise's eyes go wide, and she stands from the bed probably not expecting him to admit that in front of her. "Okay, I'm going to go. Call me when you want to go home or if you need anything," she says, waving as she walks out.

Alaska motions to the empty wall across from the bed. "You could at least have a TV in here." She groans, obviously forgetting I took my television to her place.

Well, I guess I'm ordering a television.

TWENTY-FOUR

Alaska

HE DOESN'T LET me go home until the following day, though I can't say I put up much of a fight either. It was nice to have someone care for me. I can't remember the last time I had that kind of treatment. Or if I have ever had it, for that matter.

Zuko is standing at my door, one of my bags that Louise brought over clutched in his hand.

"I'll bring the TV over," he offers. I fight the smirk on my lips. He brought me the television yesterday from his house so I wasn't bored.

"It's yours. Leave it in there."

"I don't watch TV."

"You did." I saw him watching the shows I had on.

"That's because if I sat there and watched you, you would think I'm a stalker."

I laugh, and he raises a brow. "What?"

"A stalker. That's all you're worried about being perceived as? I think of a lot worse when it comes to you."

Just as he opens his mouth to respond, my phone starts ringing—my *other* phone.

I freeze and lock eyes with him.

"You have two phones?" he asks, confused, knowing full well Louise brought my phone over yesterday, and it's in the bag he is currently holding.

"Yes. Now give me my bag and leave. I don't need you to babysit me anymore." I hold out my hand to take the bag, but he doesn't pass it to me.

"Tell me where you want it, and I'll carry it in."

"It's not that heavy." I give him my best eye roll.

He steps closer until our toes are almost touching.

My phone rings again, and I groan.

"You can get that." He nods inside.

"No, it can wait."

"Why do you have two phones?" Zuko asks.

I reach for the bag and pull it from his grasp. "That's none of your business. Now, please go." His eyes flick to the bag I'm currently holding, then back to me.

"I'll be back to check on you."

"No, you won't. Go away."

"I either come back to check on you, or I find Sarah. Pick one."

Arghh. Really?

"You're bluffing."

"I am *not* a man who bluffs. Tell me *now*, or I *will* find that bitch and show her exactly how to use a knife." His words send a shiver over my body. He lifts a hand to my shoulder, and I'm not going to lie, I *will* miss his touch. It's soothed me more than he knows. And that's saying something coming from me.

It's not my love language. And the older I get, I'm starting to understand myself a little more. I tried to pinpoint a time in my life where I could work out why I hated it. But I can't; maybe it's because I never received much of it. Or maybe it's' because I simply hate it.

"You can come back if you bring me dinner. And then you can go."

"I can help you sleep," he offers.

"I slept fine last night," I remind him.

"Yeah, that's because I was touching you the whole time."

"I've gone my whole life without you, Zuko. I'll be fine." I grip the door, and my phone starts ringing again. "Goodbye." He steps back, and I shut the door in his face. Dropping the bag to the floor, I hurry over to the phone and switch it off.

"It's a nice place you have here." My body freezes at *that* voice. "I'm glad you got rid of him. He was quite the unpleasant man. Threatening to stab me." I turn to find Sarah leaning against my bedroom door with an ugly twist to her lips. Her eyes scan me up and down. "Jeff told me about what happened. Poor you. But you seem to be doing fine."

She glances at her nails and then back to me. "This is going to be fun. You really thought you had the upper hand, didn't you? That you, of all people, would win. Tell me, Alaska, when does someone like *you* ever win?" She chuckles as feet carry her to me until she is standing directly in front of me. I go to pull my hand back to hit her, but she punches me at the same time, straight in my stomach where the stitches are.

That hurt—a lot.

I double over in pain.

But as I do, I swing my arm up and hit her right between the legs. She screams and stumbles back.

"Fucking hell, I should have brought the gun." I see her white shoes step closer to me, but I run straight to my kitchen, where I know all my cutlery is located, including the knives. Ripping open the drawer, I find one straight away and wrap my fingers around the handle. When I spin back toward her, she's at the door.

"Toodles, bitch." She pulls the door open and runs. As soon as I know she's gone, I stumble to the door, knife still clutched in my hand, and check outside. With no sign of her, I shut and lock the door.

Sarah has never been one to scare me—I'm pretty sure I could beat her ass—but what I didn't expect from her was that she plays dirty.

Collapsing onto the floor in front of the door, I lay my head on my bag, and somehow, I fall back asleep.

Something is pushing me.

I jolt awake, and the knife I was holding clangs onto the floor.

"Alaska."

Relief washes over me at the sound of Zuko's deep voice saying my name.

"Why are you against the fucking door?"

I manage to move just a little, and he squeezes his way in. His black shoes come into view, and he notices me cradling my stomach, so he crouches down and removes my hand. "Fucking hell." He shakes his head. "I leave you for a few hours to run some errands and get you food, and I come back to this."

Before I can say anything, his arms circle around me, and he lifts and carries me to my couch. After gently putting me down, he pulls my shirt up without even asking and removes the bandage. "I need to rebandage it. Stay still." I didn't realize I was moving until he said the words. Taking a deep breath, I nod and tip my head back. "Do you plan to tell me who did this? Or are you going to make me guess?" he asks.

"Who do you think did it?" I bite back.

"Why did you let her in?"

I shake my head. "She was in here already."

"So she waited for you."

"It appears so," I say dully. "This is *all* your fault, you know that, right? You got her fired, and now I have to deal with the damn consequences of that. Thanks very much!"

"I know where she lives." My eyes find him at his declaration. "Did you forget what I do, Trouble?" He smirks. "I know where she is." I go to sit up, but he pushes me back down. "And you aren't going fucking anywhere."

"Well, bring her to me, then," I snap.

"That can't happen either. I would be a fool to put someone in front of you who wants to hurt you."

A knock at the door has Zuko pulling my shirt down and standing. "Stay there. I'll get it." He walks with determination to the door and pulls it open.

Kyson enters, and his eyes find mine before they quickly go back to his brother. He leans in and whispers something to Zuko. Then Zuko nods and comes back to me, where I'm lying on the couch. "You'll stay there. You can't risk tearing those stitches open again. You've already almost succeeded."

"That wasn't my fault," I argue.

"That's fair. But stay here… Kyson will sit with you until I return."

Kyson is still standing near the door, seeming bored and checking his phone.

"I don't need a babysitter."

"I beg to differ." Zuko leans down and kisses the top of my head. "Stay here, and don't move." My gaze follows him as he approaches his brother and says something to him, then walks out the door.

I drop my head back onto the couch pillow and pick up the other one and scream into it.

I was meant to have a normal life.

Eventually, at least.

Or whatever is considered normal.

Instead, I have a complete and utter bitch after me, I'm fucking a serial killer, and now I'm being babysat by someone who probably wants to kill me as well.

I scream again, and the pillow is torn from my grasp. My eyes fly open to find Kyson staring down at me.

I growl at him. "Give me back my pillow."

"I can't let you suffocate yourself. My brother would kill me. And trust me, he knows several ways to make it hurt a lot more than it should." He moves to the single recliner and sits, pulling out his phone again and playing a noisy game. I give him my best fuck-you glare, which doesn't even phase him.

Attempting to get up, I manage to get to my feet. But when I lift my head, Kyson is now in front of me.

"What are you doing?" I ask.

He's stopping me from even moving one inch.

"You aren't allowed to walk, so sit back down. If you need something, ask."

"Why are you all so bossy?" I groan. "I can walk to my own kitchen and get my own shit."

"No, you can't. Now… What. Do. You. Need?"

"I'm not telling you." I cross my arms over my chest.

"Well, you aren't moving either," he says, still blocking my path. We stand there, eye-to-eye, and I know he isn't going to give in. He clearly has orders from his brother, and he doesn't seem like one to go against Zuko.

I wonder why.

"Do you always take orders?"

"I don't take orders."

"But you do, from your brother," I push.

"That's not the same. He's blood. It's not an order from him. It's a suggestion. But he will fuck you up if you don't listen." He winks. "Do you plan to get fucked-up today?" I check my clothes, running my eyes down my body.

"I'm already fucked-up," I whine.

"Touché. I guess you are." He laughs. "Now, what do you need? And sit down like a well-behaved woman and tell me."

"I need painkillers." He nods and locks eyes with me, and I notice he and Zuko have the same color eyes, except Kyson's seem a little darker. "And water."

"Okay. Now sit."

I do as he says and slowly lower myself back on the couch. Sliding the pillow behind my back so I'm not bent over, he watches me do it before he heads into the kitchen.

"Am I the first girl he's instructed you to watch?" I yell.

"No."

Hmm...

"What was the last one's name?" I ask. "Is it a pattern for him?" He comes back with a glass of water and pills in one hand. After he offers them to me, I place them in my mouth and take the water.

"There was one other. Actually, I think she died from an overdose of pills that I *may* have given her." My eyes go wide. "Joking. Zuko doesn't keep nor care about women. Like most bachelors, he fucks 'em and leaves 'em."

"Or fucks them to kill them," I add.

"Oh, yes, he does like some fucked-up shit." He smirks. "But you're still alive and still here, so it can't be that bad for you."

"It's fucked-up."

"I bet you enjoyed it."

I don't bother replying to that, and he sits back down and picks up his phone.

"When are you leaving?" I ask after a few silent minutes.

"Once Zuko has hunted his prey." He smirks, and the twinkle in his eye tells me he is one fucked-up son of a bitch. "Sometimes, he likes to play with them a little longer than necessary."

Jesus! A shiver breaks over me at his words.

TWENTY-FIVE

Zuko

SARAH ISN'T the smartest bitch in the world, that's for sure, but I didn't think she would be hard to find.

When I do find her, she's sitting at a restaurant with the manager of the bar, Jeff. She leans in and reaches for his hand, gripping it. He smiles at her, and I wonder… *No.* He wouldn't be *that* stupid.

Stepping up to me, the server takes one look and walks the other way. I make my way over to them, stopping when I reach their table. Jeff's head tilts up when he senses someone next to him, and surprise is written all over his face when he sees me.

"Zuko."

I nod to him and turn my focus to Sarah, who bites her lip as she avoids eye contact with me.

"Can I join you?" I ask, but I don't wait for a reply as I pull out a chair and sit directly between them at the table. They are sitting opposite each other, and Sarah pulls her hand back and tucks it in her lap.

"How are you?" Jeff asks.

"Good. Actually, I just came from Alaska's."

Sarah tenses at my words and I don't miss her body language, but I keep my eyes on Jeff.

"Oh, yes, how is she?" he asks. "I tried checking the cameras to find out who attacked her, and all I could see was someone wearing a black hoodie." He shakes his head.

"She's fine, resting at her place at the moment. Seems she got an unexpected visitor."

Jeff looks at me, confused.

"Was the attack personal, you think? I mean, you do that stuff, right? Find people?"

"I do. Not many people have evaded me... Actually none." I turn and look at Sarah while she chews on her bottom lip.

"Would you mind getting me a coffee, Jeff?" He stands without a second thought, pushing his seat back and walking over to the counter.

"Is she okay?" she asks, but there is no concern in her voice whatsoever.

"She will be," I answer. Leaning forward, I place my hands on the table. "Do you really care?" I raise a brow at her and tilt my head.

Sarah chews her bottom lip again and looks past me, more than likely hoping Jeff will save her.

That's not going to happen.

"Do you know who I am?" I ask when she doesn't reply, and her eyes shoot back to mine.

"You find people. That's what you just said." Venom laces her tone, and I can tell she doesn't like me.

"Have you heard of the Hunter brothers?" Her brows pinch together, and then her eyes go wide. "Yes, I think you have."

Jeff walks back, and I stand and throw a twenty on the table. "Something came up, so I have to go. Enjoy the coffee." I nod to him and turn to Sarah. "I'll be seeing you *real* soon." I wink at her and walk off.

Sarah goes back to her house, which is a stupid move. I watch as she locks the door and flicks on the lights. She proceeds to kick off her shoes as she makes her way to the kitchen, not once looking in my direction.

When she pulls open the refrigerator door, I say, "I'd like a glass of milk, please." She freezes, her head spinning around until she finds me sitting at her table, a knife playing in one of my hands while the other rests on the table's surface. Her snake-like eyes spot the knife straight away, and she quickly goes to her cutlery drawer to pull out one of her own.

"That's what Alaska did, right?" I ask when she opens it and sees it's empty.

Panic sets in, and she backs up until her ass hits the stove behind her. "Get out of my house," she orders shakily.

I stand as my phone rings. Seeing my brother's name, I answer it, but it's Alaska's voice that comes through.

"Where are you? I don't want your babysitter anymore," she whines into the phone.

"Give me my phone back." I hear Kyson say.

"No, fuck off," she screams, and I hear movement. "Where are you, Zuko?"

I put the phone on speaker and step closer to Sarah, placing the phone on the counter. Then I reach into my pocket and pull out a pair of gloves, slowly slipping them on.

Her eyes watch my every move as I carry out each one in meticulous slow detail.

"Answer me!" Alaska growls.

"Don't you come any closer," Sarah warns.

"Who was that? Zuko, so help me, God, you better answer me. Why is there another woman with you?"

"She isn't with me. I came to show her who *not* to fuck with."

"Sarah," Alaska says.

Sarah's eyes flick to the phone but quickly come back to me. "Tell your deranged boyfriend to *get out of my house*, you whore."

"Like the way you got out of mine?" Alaska yells.

"At least be a woman and handle it yourself. Don't get your fucked-up boyfriend to do it for you," Sarah screams, backing away as I stalk toward her.

"He isn't my boyfriend, you silly cunt." Alaska grunts, and I know she just hurt herself.

"What am I, then?" I ask Alaska but keep my eyes on Sarah.

"This is not the time, and you are nothing but

an annoying man who tries to kill me when you fuck me."

I smirk at her words.

"And I plan to burn your house down," she adds.

"You and burning my house down. I would have thought you would be over that by now," I say.

Sarah's eyes keep flicking between the phone and me like she can't believe what we're saying.

"You need to leave," Sarah demands. She goes to run, but I manage to grab her. She erupts in a scream, but I shove a rag in her mouth, effectively shutting her the fuck up.

"What's going on?" Alaska asks frantically. "Do you have her?"

"Yes." I hit the side of Sarah's head, and she drops like a piece of shit to the floor. I reach for the zip ties in my back pocket and tie her hands behind her. Rolling her, so she's facing upward, I go back to my phone. "Trouble, I have to go now."

"No!" she yells. "Do *not* kill her!"

"Goodbye, Trouble." I whistle out a sigh.

"Fuck yo—"

I hang up, effectively cutting off her scream.

TWENTY-SIX

Alaska

"I WILL KICK you in the balls if you do not tell me where he is." I glare at Kyson, who's holding his hand out for his phone. I press call again, but Zuko doesn't answer. *Asshole.* Of course he doesn't answer. "I have a good aim," I warn.

"Not happening." He tries to take his phone again, but as I end the call, I check it and smile as I navigate to the Find My iPhone function. *They wouldn't have it on, surely?* But then, just as I see Zuko's name pop up and the street he is on, I know they do. I throw Kyson's phone at him and head to the door, reaching for my keys as Kyson reaches me. I push past him and out the door.

"I will carry your ass back through that door. Don't you fucking make me," he threatens.

"How mad at you do you think he will get if he hears you hurt me?"

"You can't track him. You only saw a street, so how will you narrow it down?" He smiles as if he's got me.

"I'm not going there. I'm going somewhere else."

I stroll to my car, and he follows. Kyson holds open the passenger door for me to get in, and as soon as the door is closed, I lock it and climb over to the other side, grunting as I hurt my stomach. I start the car as Kyson leans down to my window and shakes his head. He doesn't have the spare keys on him—I saw them on the table when we walked out. He pats his pockets as if he realizes this as well and then bangs on my window.

Ha! Yeah, that's not going to happen.

I press call from my phone to Zuko's, but not from my private phone number, from Sage's. He answers, and I hear noises in the background.

"You're calling me," he states.

"I had missed calls from you," I say sweetly.

"I'm kind of busy. This isn't the time for a call from you."

"But I have something interesting to share with you." I hear a thud before it gets quieter.

"And what is that?" he asks.

"I want to show you what I look like."

"You do?" he asks, surprised. Then he adds, "Look, I have to tell you something."

"What is it?" My voice is way too sweet for how I'm feeling right now.

"I'm with someone else."

"Oh, you are?" I say, disappointment evident in my tone. "In a relationship or just fucking?" I push for more details.

"Well…" He goes quiet for a few seconds, obviously thinking about what he wants to say next. "I want to strangle her *half* the time, fuck her *most* of the time, and make sure she is okay *all* of the time." I can just imagine his hands running through his hair right now.

"I should let you go," I say softly. "Since you don't want or need me anymore, I should let you go."

"Sage…"

"Yes?"

"If I had met you first—" I hang up as I pull up to the bar. It's not open until later, but I know Jeff will be here. He's always here.

Pushing open the door at the back, I go straight to his office. I come to a complete stop when I see what's happening right in front of me. Louise is there, on her knees, in front of Jeff.

Fuck, Jeff gets around.

Lucky bastard.

"Um…"

Both of them freeze for a split second.

Then Louise hits her head on his desk as she goes to get up. When she spots me, her eyes go wide, and she stands, pulling down her skirt.

"Alaska, what are you doing here?" she asks.

"Um… What are you doing here?" I question back.

She looks at Jeff, who is tucking his cock back into his pants, and then back to me.

"I…" She shakes her head. "I don't have an explanation." She shrugs.

"I thought you were with Sarah," I ask Jeff, and his face scrunches.

"Aren't you meant to be on bed rest?" He points to my stomach. "If you can work—"

"She can't work. Her stomach was cut open, you fool," Louise says, cutting him off. "Anyway. Clearly, this was a lapse in judgment. He gave me great head, so I returned the favor."

"Still no reason to be sucking his cock."

I shiver at that thought.

It's just wrong on all levels.

Jeff is sleazy.

Louise tucks her hair behind her ear and steps away from him, and his eyes track her movements. "Where are you going?" he says, but she ignores him and comes over to me.

"Are you okay? Why are you here?"

I look past her to Jeff.

"I need Sarah's address," I tell him.

He throws his head back and laughs. "That's a joke and never happening."

"Why? Are you still fucking her too?"

"Of course I am. She plans to move in with me."

From the corner of my eye, I see Louise shake her head.

"You just told me you were broken up," she accuses.

"Well, we are. But not." He scowls. "She would still be here if it weren't for you," Jeff says, blaming me for Sarah's current situation.

Louise reaches for me. "Let's go. *I quit!*" she yells.

"Her address?" I demand.

"Not happening."

"I quit too," I announce, turning and walking out.

He starts yelling, but neither of us pays any attention.

As we step outside, Kyson's leaning against my car.

"Fuck!" I grumble.

He stares us down as we approach.

"I need you to do me a favor," I tell her.

"What?"

"Distract him." I discreetly point to Kyson.

"How?"

"I don't care. And give me the keys to your car." She hands them to me, and I give her mine. I watch as she saunters up to him, but he pays no attention to her. As soon as Louise is in front of him, she tries blocking his view, but his eyes never stray from me. She glances back at me as I near her car, which is parked a few spots in front of mine.

Shrugging, she turns back to him and lifts her skirt. I see her ass in plain view, and his eyes fall to what's below—she isn't wearing panties, and Kyson notices. I want to laugh, but instead, I climb into her car and start it. When I look up, I see him stalking my way, so I quickly pull out and take off, flipping him off. And as I speed by, he yells something at me. When I check the rearview mirror, I see Louise laughing as he passes her on his way to his car.

Putting my focus back on the road, I know what will get Zuko's attention.

And he may not like it.

But fuck him.

He chose not to listen to me, and payback is always a bitch.

And that bitch is me.

TWENTY-SEVEN

Zuko

"WHAT DO YOU MEAN, you lost her?" I growl into the phone.

"Well, she ran the first time, and I found her. Then…" Kyson trails off.

"Then what?" I snap.

"Well, she got her friend to distract me. She's looking for you."

"She won't find me," I tell him. "But *you* better fucking find *her*."

"I'm not your personal babysitter," he yells. "You should have asked Kenzo."

"No, I asked you. So go, do your job, and *find her*."

"I'm not getting paid enough for this," he grumbles.

"I'm not paying you at all. Just do it."

He hangs up, and I look over to Sarah, who is starting to wake up. My legs are crossed as I sit on the recliner directly across from where she's tied to a chair in the middle of her living room. She blinks a few times as if she can't believe what's happening.

She better believe it.

She starts to scream, but I already have a rag stuffed in her mouth, so nothing comes out but muffled sounds. I sit calmly, watching her. When she finally stops screaming, realizing it's not getting her anywhere, she starts to pull against the restraints.

Again, getting nowhere.

When she finally settles and her breathing becomes heavier, I stand and pull the rag from her mouth.

"If you scream, I'm either going to knock you out again or stuff this back in your mouth. Your choice." When she doesn't speak or move, I sit back down and rest my ankle on my opposite knee as I study her.

"Why are you here?" she asks in a small voice.

I smirk, my head tilting to the side. "Do you think acting innocent will help you?" I raise a brow.

Her lips thin, and her brows scrunch. She pulls on the restraints, but it gets her nowhere.

"I also figured I would give you the same surprise you gave Alaska. Nice, right? I thought, how romantic is this." I wave my hands around in front of me. "You surprised her in her home, and I am doing the same." I watch as she bites the inside of her lip.

"I won't—" she starts and stops herself.

"You won't what?" I ask. "Tell me a lie, and I'll cut a finger off." I smile at her.

My phone starts ringing again, but I ignore it keeping my attention pinned on Sarah.

"Why did you stab her?" I ask.

"Because she *cost me my job*!" she shouts.

"That was only half the truth. Tell me the whole truth."

"I did tell you the whole truth."

"Losing a job doesn't mean you go and stab someone. Technically, she didn't get you fired... *I did*. Would you like to stab me as well?"

"Yes, I *very* much would," she bites back.

"See? The truth helps you keep your body parts." I wink at her. "Now, tell me why you *really* did it."

She clenches her jaw, then whines, "I told you why."

I stand, the knife that was hidden in my lap now

in my hand. Her eyes widen when she notices it, and she struggles against the rope, but it gets her nowhere. Of course it won't, silly girl.

"What are you doing? I told you the truth. What are you doing?" she repeats. I smile as I reach for one of her hands, which are tied behind her back. She tries her hardest to pull them free and wiggles them as much as she possibly can.

But that's not going to work, not with me.

Holding out her pinkie, I grip it before setting the blade of my knife against it.

Despite what people think, you actually need to put in some effort when you're slicing a bone from the body. Her screams rip through the room as her blood drips into a small puddle at my feet. I manage to cut through all the way and hold the pinkie between my fingers. I pull the rag from my pocket and tie it around her hand, and she screams at the contact. I move back to the recliner and sit down, still holding her pinkie finger firmly.

"You had to go and make it hard…" I pause, looking up at her. "For you, that is." I throw her finger at her, and it hits her chest, then falls to the floor in front of her. "Now, care to tell me again why you are being a bitch and hurting Alaska?"

Tears have streaked her mascara down her face,

and she lifts her shoulder and attempts to wipe it away but doesn't get far.

"I'm not a patient man," I tell her.

"What do you see in her?" she asks. "She's so ordinary."

"Now, you don't believe that, do you?" As she goes to open her mouth, I hold up a finger before I point to her pinkie on the floor. "Remember…the truth now, please."

She bites her lip, tears still rolling down her face. "I'm a woman. How could you do this to me?"

"You are the one who decided to be a cunt. Remember that? Don't try playing the victim card with me. I couldn't give two shits that you're a woman. You could be a man for all I care." She shakes her head, trying to dispel the tears streaming down her face.

"I'm jealous! Jealous of her! Are you happy now?" she yells.

"Was that *really* so hard?" I question. "Telling the truth isn't so difficult, is it?" I smile as I stand, and my brother calls again for the fourth time. "Alaska is a sweet woman. She wouldn't hurt you the same way you hurt her, despite her tough exterior," I tell her, putting the phone to my ear.

Sarah laughs and shakes her head, tears still

welling in her eyes. "She is anything but," she snarls.

"Your house is on fire! Why haven't you been answering your fucking phone?" Kyson screams.

"My what?" I say, not sure I heard him right.

"Your crazy lover just set your house on fire. Next time answer your phone. She is as crazy as you. Fucking hell, I'm leaving. I hear sirens coming and I am not waiting around for consequences."

"Take her with you," I order.

"Fuck off," my brother says and hangs up the phone.

Turning back to Sarah, I approach her slowly, the knife still in my hand. She jolts at seeing the blade come near her, and I smile and lean down, then cut the ties that bind her hands.

"It's your lucky day. I have to go. And remember, if you go near her again, you'll lose more than one finger." I pull back and slide the knife into its sheath. When she doesn't answer, I step closer and bend down, my menacing eyes focusing directly on hers. "Do. You. Understand?" I ask, my words coming out as a growl.

She nods emphatically, and I ruffle her hair before I stride out.

TWENTY-EIGHT

Alaska

HA, *take that, bitch.*

Hands wrap around me as heat licks my face. They are careful not to touch my stomach as they lift me.

"Put me down," I shout.

"Fuck! Are you trying to get us locked up? You're fucking crazy." I laugh at Kyson's words and smile as I look back to the house.

Zuko's house.

Which is now up in flames.

That's what he gets.

I didn't give him permission to take matters into his own hands and go crazy on someone.

Granted, she deserved it, but still.

I wanted to deal with it myself.

I didn't ask him to go all macho and handle *my* stuff. I'm a strong, independent woman and can do that shit by myself, thank you very much.

"Put me down," I tell Kyson again as we reach his car.

"No. Get the fuck in the car. I don't want to be locked up today." He places me in the back seat of the car as the sirens get closer. "You better not fucking run again," he warns. I smile at him, and he shakes his head as he gets into the front seat and starts the engine. As soon as he is about to take off, I jump out of the car.

That was a really stupid mistake.

Because it burns.

A lot.

Fucking hell! I wince and glance back at Kyson. He gives me a murderous glare before he drives off.

I sit on the grass in front of the house as I watch it burn. Firefighters rush to put the flames out as neighbors come to see what's happening. One person asks me if I'm okay, and I look down to see my shirt has blood on it. *Great.* Lifting my head, I watch as the fire is put out, but everything inside is burned.

Ha, take that asshole.

"Are you enjoying the show?" I stiffen as Zuko

stops in front of me, his hands hanging loosely at his sides and sunglasses covering his eyes.

"Yes, very much so." I give him a smug smile.

"You set my house on fire," he states.

"Look at you, Captain Obvious." I laugh, and it hurts when I do. *Fuck this stomach wound.*

He bends down, so we are eye-to-eye. "Why?"

"I warned you time and time again. It's not my fault you chose not to listen." I shrug. He lifts his sunglasses so I can see his eyes. They stare back at me, and I have to remember to breathe.

"Fair point," he replies.

"What did you do to her?" I ask. "You better not have killed her. Because if you did, I'm going to do much worse next."

Zuko fights a smirk before he shakes his head and scoffs. "What do you plan to do, Trouble?"

"I'll find something else you love to set on fire," I snap. "Why are you smirking?"

"Because that's funny. I've never loved anything in this life."

I'm shocked at his words, so I cover it and point to the house. "You didn't love your house?"

"Nope. If you noticed, there was nothing personal in there. Though I am disappointed, I have to shop again…for *everything*. I fucking hate shopping, especially for clothes."

"I love shopping for clothes," I mention as two police officers approach us.

Zuko stands, and they ask him what happened. He lies and says he was asleep and left a candle too close to a curtain, that it was too late by the time he woke, and that he barely made it outside, then he heard sirens.

I sit there as he tells a perfectly crafted lie.

The officers stare down at me for a moment, and then their attention turns back to Zuko.

"So, accidental?" they ask.

"Yep. No insurance would accept this. So I guess I'll just have to rebuild myself." They nod, happy with that, then write down a few particulars on their notepads.

"That will go into the report. So if you change your mind, the insurance company will see this," one of them says.

"I get that," he states, his tone bored and unconcerned. They seem taken aback by him. Both are standing a distance away from him, and they give him a nod before they turn and step off.

"Do I need to carry you, or can you walk?" Zuko asks, looming above me. I roll my eyes and stand. I try my best not to show any pain when I stand, but I must admit I am walking a little funny.

"You didn't answer me," I tell him as he holds open the car door. "Where did Louise's car go?" I ask, scanning the area.

"I had it taken back to her. Nice job evading my brother, by the way. He is fucking pissed."

I smile. "It was fun."

Zuko shuts the door and strolls around to the driver's side, then slides in. Starting the car, he drives off.

"Now, tell me what you did. Is she at least still alive?"

He nods to the glove compartment, and I eye it suspiciously.

"Open it." I do as he says and see a black rag, so I pull it out, and as I do, something drops in my lap. When I check between my legs, I see a pale object. When I grab it, it feels squishy. Inspecting it closer, I scream and shift back in the seat, trying to escape the obvious and letting it drop back between my legs.

I try to climb away from it, and Zuko swears before he pulls the car over, slamming on the brakes and reaching for the finger. *A fucking finger!* He wraps it back in the rag and places it back in the glove compartment before he turns to me.

"Calm down. You'll hurt yourself."

I take a deep breath and manage to sit my ass back down. "That was a finger," I state, my eyes wide.

"It was," he confirms unnecessarily.

"It was Sarah's?"

He nods.

"And where is the rest of Sarah?"

He repositions himself behind the wheel and pulls back out onto the road. "Still breathing. *For now.*"

"Where is she?" I ask again.

"Probably cleaning up her hand. She does bleed a lot."

"Why did you cut her finger off?"

He gives me a side-eye. "Why did she stab you?" he asks, raising a brow.

"Because she's crazy," I reply. "Doesn't mean I want her dead."

"I do," he answers. Then, with more force, he adds, "For touching you, she deserves what she gets. And more."

"You are *not* to kill her. Do you understand?"

He clenches his jaw. Eyes still trained on the

road. "No one tells me what to do. That is one of the joys of being me."

"Stop the car," I demand.

He ignores me and keeps on driving.

"Stop the car, Zuko. If you think you can do what you please in my life, and I don't have a say about it, you are dead wrong. So *stop the fucking car,* and I *will* walk." I see his hands gripping the steering wheel tighter as he turns the steering wheel, and we pull up to a house.

Kyson comes out the front door, and when he spots me sitting in the car, he shakes his head. Zuko gets out and storms up to him, and in one swift movement, he knocks him straight out. Kyson falls backward and hits the ground. Hard. Zuko turns and walks back to the car. Not saying a word, he starts it again and tears out of the driveway.

"You just hit your brother," I say, appalled.

"Yes. He had one job, and he failed multiple times." He flexes his fingers, working his knuckles. "He's lucky he is still breathing."

He speeds down the streets until we come to a strip of shops. He pulls into a parking spot and turns to look at me. "You like to shop, so you can help me."

"Ha!" I roll my eyes. "Do you pick and choose what you want to listen to?"

"Oh, I listen to you. It's hard for me not to, even when I don't want to." He gets out of the car, walks around to my side, and opens the door. "She's alive, and she will stay that way as long as she stays away from you. How is that for *listening*," he says emphasizing the word and offering me his hand.

"You are a real ass," I tell him.

"I already knew that, and so did you. So let's shop." I take his offered hand and get out. He clasps my hand in his and starts walking to the shops. He heads straight for the men's store and looks at everything. I can see the pain on his face, and I want to laugh. A big scary man afraid of shopping. How cliché.

"How can I help you today?" a sales assistant asks. He didn't just walk into your average Target. No, he stepped into a designer store. I'm not even sure he knows that, but he will once he pays.

"She's picking my clothes."

The woman glances at me and smiles.

"Anything in particular? Shirts? A hat, perhaps?" she inquires.

"Everything. I need everything." He sighs.

The sales assistant's eyes light up. It will be a

nice bonus for her today. She offers us a glass of champagne. I take one and, before it hits my lips, he swipes it from me and hands it back. "She will have orange juice."

The sales lady's eyes flick between Zuko and me, and then she quietly retreats to get my juice.

"Why did you do that?" I park my hands on my hips.

"You are on medication that can't be mixed with alcohol," he states.

Oh, yeah, I forgot about that.

"You aren't the boss of me," I tell him. "In fact, I don't like you at all."

"Liar," he says, his voice low and sexy, as the sales lady brings out a glass of orange juice. I take it from her and drink it before I sit down. Zuko sits next to me as she displays all the clothes in front of us. I'm too in tune with how close he is to fully concentrate.

She asks him if he would like any color other than black, to which he replies with a simple, "No." She says something else, but it all jumbles together as his hand lands on my thigh and squeezes. My eyes are glued to his hand.

"Trouble." I look up at him through my eyelashes and see a soft smile on his lips.

"It's the medication," I explain. His lips fight a smirk as his eyes search mine.

"I'm sure it is. Now, do you want anything?"

When I look away from him, I see the lady smiling at me, waiting for me to answer.

"I—" Before I can even finish, she brings two things out from behind her—black boots that are snug on the ankle and a matching bag—and a huge grin lights up my face.

"We'll take them as well. Bag it all up, please." Her expression shows how happy she is. I'm not sure Zuko will be once he knows the price tag on those boots, or that bag, for that matter.

But will he care? a small part of me asks.

"Trouble." He grips my thigh and places a finger under my chin, turning my head, so I'm facing him. I grind my molars as my eyes slowly lift to meet his. "I really like you, Trouble."

"I bet you say that to all the girls," I taunt as I feel my cheeks redden.

"No, in fact, I don't. There was one girl who was close."

"Who?" I ask as his fingers stroke my jaw.

"You wouldn't know her." He stands, his fingers falling away from my face, then offers me his hand to help me up.

"Do you still talk to her?"

"Why? If I said yes, would you attempt to burn something else down?"

"What do you have left?" I ask sassily as we head to the counter.

"I'm afraid to tell you." He smirks.

I nudge his shoulder with mine as we reach the counter. "Come on...tell me."

He locks his gaze on mine as the sales lady rings up the items. When she says the total, he hands her his black card without even glancing her way, his eyes solely on me.

"The only thing that would affect me, as you have seen, is you getting hurt." At first, I want to smile at that, but then I remember how he likes to fuck. My mouth drops into a frown, and he notices straight away.

"What?" he asks.

Raising a brow at him, I tell him what's in my thoughts.

"What about the bag?" I don't want to freak the lady out by asking about the knife, but I'm sure he gets it.

"If that really does bother you as much as you say it does, I won't do it again."

Zuko picks up the bags, and we leave the shop.

"That's not fair to you; it's clearly your kink."

"Why wouldn't it be fair to me?"

We get to the car, and he puts all the bags in the back before he comes and opens my door.

"We aren't a thing. You get that, right?" I stand in the space between the door and the seat, and he steps closer until he is almost touching me. But he's careful not to.

"We aren't?" He raises a brow in question.

"No, we are *not*. To be a thing, two people have to agree."

"I agree for both of us," he informs me, not even joking.

"Ha!" I give him an unimpressed look and get in the car. He shuts my door, rounds the hood, and climbs in. "Where are we going?" I ask.

"Home," he informs me as he starts the car.

"Just in case you've forgotten, you don't have a home anymore." I can't help but say it with a smile.

"Oh, I know. I have a new one."

"Already?" I reply, surprised.

"Yes, and we should be arriving soon." I'm amazed he is even going to take me there, especially after what I did. But when we pull down a familiar street, I turn to face him.

"This isn't the way." I stare out the window as

my apartment comes into view. "Oh God, did you buy one on my block?"

"Nope." He brings the car to a stop and then turns to me.

"Why are we here?" I'm afraid of the answer.

"Because I'm moving in. Now, do you need help getting out of the car?" he asks casually, and I can't seem to pick my jaw up to close my mouth.

TWENTY-NINE

Zuko

I WAIT for her at the car door.

She doesn't want to move, but she doesn't have a choice.

She either sits in the car or goes into the house.

"You aren't moving in with me." She crosses her arms over her chest.

"You should have thought about that before you set my house on fire." I go to the back of the car and retrieve the bags, and then I return to her. "Now, come in and show me where to put my shit."

She groans as she stands and slams the car door shut behind her. "I did not agree to this. I want that noted."

"Noted," I tell her as I walk up to her front door. She unlocks it and goes straight in. I stand

238

there as she picks up a few things and then stops to stare at the floor. *Fuck, I forgot to clean up her blood.* "Your room?" I ask, trying to distract her from the stain on the floor.

"Nope. You can sleep on the couch." She points to it, holding a bag in her other hand. She goes to a small cupboard and pulls out a blanket and throws it on the couch before she faces me again. "No sneaking into my bed," she warns.

"You like it when I'm in your bed," I remind her.

"I do not."

"If you say so." I drop my things and stroll into the kitchen, opening the refrigerator. It's partially empty, aside from a few things like condiments. "Do you not cook?"

"Nope. I know how to make one thing. And even that is not really cooking." She smiles sweetly.

"What can you make?" I ask.

She comes up next to me and grabs a container from the refrigerator. Popping the lid off, she shows me what's inside—it's cream. A lot of cream, to be precise.

"My chocolate cake. I have a sweet tooth, and this is fast and easy." I lift it to my nose and sniff—it smells all right. She reaches for a fork and hands it to me.

"Will it poison me?" I sniff it again.

"No, it's amazing. It would make any grown man want to marry me for that cake alone." She smirks.

"Marry you?" I say, surprised. "Well, I've never wanted to marry anyone in my life, so let's see if this cake changes that." I dig the fork in, then pull it back out. It's layered with cream and chocolate. She stands there with a smile on her face as she watches me put it to my lips. As soon as it hits my tongue, I can taste multiple flavors. Obviously, chocolate, the sweetness of the cream, but something a little sour too.

Swallowing, I eye her.

"No, I will not marry you," she says, triumph in her voice. She spins on her heel and walks away.

"What's the sour part?" I call after her.

"There are three ingredients. If you can guess all three, I'll let you wash me."

Well, holy shit.

I will take that and run.

Shutting the refrigerator after I place the cake back inside, I follow her to where she went down the hall.

"Chocolate cookies," I state the first.

"Bingo."

"Cream."

"Correct. You're so close. But can you guess the last ingredient?" She grabs the hem of her shirt, holding it up, ready to pull it off. "You only get *one guess*." I stand directly in front of her. Leaning down, so I'm near her ear, I whisper, "Orange juice."

She pulls back, and her eyes narrow at me. "How did you know?"

"It's all you have in your fridge, Trouble. It was that or eggs. And I wonder if you even know how to cook an egg."

"I do not, thank you very much," she says, a teasing light behind her eyes.

Spinning around, she crosses into her room. "Are you coming?" she asks. I follow her in and watch as she starts tearing her clothes from her body. When she reaches the shower, she turns it on and steps in. "It already has a waterproof bandage on it." I nod as if she can read my mind.

When she steps under the water, I take her in. Alaska's body is no different from a lot of women I have seen, but it's not only her body that has me coming back, or more accurately, that I can't stay away from—*literally can't stay away from*—it's that her hips are flared, and she's shaped like a pin-up girl. It's pure perfection. Her ass is round, but not from years of working out. No, it's perfection just as is.

"Do you plan to shower with me or just watch?"

"I'm happy watching."

"Who's going to wash my back?" She turns, giving me her back.

"You don't want me in there," I tell her. "You burned my house down because you don't like me, remember?"

"No, I burned it down to teach you that you clearly have control issues, and I am not one of those things you can control." She turns around, grabs the loofah, and starts washing her body. "I'm tired. Either come in here and help or—"

"Or what?"

She sighs and turns back around.

I tear off my shirt and throw it to the floor before I follow with the rest of my clothing. When I step in, and the hot water hits my skin, I try not to wince. "How can you have it this hot?"

"It's not *that* hot." She laughs. Turning to face me, she lifts the loofah and puts it on my chest. "You really have the perfect body." I look down as she moves it across my pecs.

"Did you miss the scars I have?" I ask, nodding to the one she is currently touching.

"I like them. They make your god-like body seem more…" she pauses, "real." Her other hand touches my lower stomach, and I know she doesn't miss it when my cock twitches at her touch. "Tell me something real," she whispers. "I sometimes think you are a figment of my imagination, something you read about in fiction books. I mean, you are all types of fucked-up, but I see glimpses that make it hard for me to stay away."

"Don't run away," I tell her, pulling her to me. She comes easily and lays both her hands on my chest.

"It's easier that way… to protect my heart," she almost whispers, but I hear her all the same.

"Kenzo gave me that scar," I tell her, nodding to where her hand is on my chest. "He got high, and I mean very high on some drugs that one of the guys slipped him. And, well, he was tripping hard and stabbed me with my own knife."

"Did you do anything to him?"

"Yeah, I knocked him out. He slept off the drugs."

She chuckles and hands me the loofah. "I've never been in love either," she confesses something real with me as I run the loofah over her arm. She peeks down at my hard cock but says nothing. Let's be honest, it's not going anywhere knowing she's here. "I'm not even sure I want to be in love. Love makes people do crazy things, and I prefer sex." As she says that last part, her finger ghosts over the tip of my cock before she wraps her hand around it gently and squeezes.

"Sex is always fun." I grunt when she starts to stroke me.

"Your type of sex is *not* fun." While licking her lips, she locks her eyes on mine.

"If I recall, you came every time." I leave those words hanging there.

"And it scared the shit out of me."

"A little punishment or pain in fucking is always fun," I confess while her hand is still working my cock.

"I think you should kiss me now." She tips her head up, and I waste no time, lifting my hands to her face and gripping it as my lips meet hers. Kissing Alaska is like entering a storm—it's pretty to look at, but once you are in the middle of it, you can't see any way to escape. She's a storm to me, and I get sucked in every time. Since the first moment I laid eyes on her, I knew I wanted her. She has something about her that simply drew me in. I can't even pinpoint precisely what it is, but it's one hundred percent her.

Her lips move against mine, touching and tasting me. I can't seem to stop myself as I hold her face tighter and take in all that she is.

"Zuko…" she mumbles against my lips, "the water has gone cold." She pulls her mouth from mine, her hand drops from my chest, and she smiles as she steps out of the shower.

I move under the cold water to try to help my hard cock, but it does nothing to stop the strain.

Of her.

THIRTY

Alaska

AFTER THE SHOWER, I went to my room and didn't come out. Zuko didn't attempt to come in last night either.

I woke up this morning feeling better, like I can move now without wanting to cry. When I get up and leave my room, I find him in the kitchen wearing nothing but a pair of basketball shorts. He eyes me from over his shoulder as I make my way to him.

"This is the best my kitchen has ever smelled," I tell him.

"You do know you shouldn't store shoes in the oven?" he questions.

"I ran out of room everywhere else." I shrug

and notice he's cooking an omelet in one pan and bacon in the other.

"Where did you get the fry pans from?"

"You really don't have anything in this place. How do you survive?"

I step over to the freezer and pull it open to show him my frozen dinners. "Quick and easy." I smile, closing the door.

"You're looking better." His eyes assess me. I am wearing a nightie, one that's loose enough it doesn't cling to my skin so I can move without it hurting.

"I feel better," I reply. "You cooked enough for me too, right?"

"This is all for you. I ate already." He gets a plastic plate from the cabinet, and I can't help but laugh at the face he pulls. He says nothing and starts to plate up the food while I watch him with interest.

Who is this man?

I mean, I think I know him.

But then he shows me glimpses of another side of him and I wonder how much you can ever know a man.

"I have a favor to ask you," he says.

"Hmm…" I mumble as he places the food in front of me. "Is that why you cooked?"

"No, I cooked because you clearly are missing substance in your meals." He nods to it. "And protein."

"I like to get my protein another way." I smirk. "How much would you say is in a man's cum?" I question. If looks could make you drop your skirt, the one he's giving me right now would do it. His lashes lift, and ever so slowly, his eyes find mine. I've heard of smolder before, but I've never actually witnessed it—*until now.*

This man knows how to smolder.

"I have a dinner to attend tonight, but it's a weird dinner. I wouldn't ask you to go, but I don't want to leave you alone. My brothers and Pops will be there. And I trust no one else with your safety but me."

"Safety?" I question, with a mouth full of eggs.

"Yes."

"You think Sarah will try again? I mean, you did cut her finger off," I remind him.

She wouldn't be that stupid, right? Even if she is *really* stupid.

"Will you come?"

"What do I wear? And is it a date?" My lips curve up into a wide smile.

"You'll wear a masquerade mask to hide who

you are. No one is to know your identity at this party. If they ask for your name, you'll give them a fake one."

"Mmm… okay."

"This is not a joke," he says seriously, reaching over and gripping my hand. "I need you to repeat to me that you will *not* tell anyone your name."

I nod my head and pick up a piece of bacon. "Okay, okay. I get it."

"I have a dress being delivered soon. And a mask to match."

"What if I don't like it?" I keep on chewing the delicious bacon, nothing beats that crunch and salty flavor.

"You will." He starts to clean up and huffs when he doesn't find what he's after.

The doorbell rings, and before I can get up to answer, he's already there, opening the door and reaching out for something. He shuts the door and returns with two garment bags and places one of the bags on the counter next to me. I wipe my hands on my nightie and unzip the bag so I can see my dress.

It's black with lace around the bodice and a Cinderella-like skirt. I run my hand along the silk and smile up at him.

"It's beautiful, especially considering how much you hate shopping. You chose well."

"It's nothing special. I did it online," he replies, carrying the other garment bag, which I assume to be his suit, to the couch. He places it down and grabs something before he heads to the shower. I hear the water turn on, and it takes everything in me not to go and join him. Instead, I sit there finishing my breakfast and staring at the dress.

When I hear the shower turn off, I look up to watch him walk out with a towel around his waist.

"I've asked your friend to come over and stay with you. I have to do some work today."

"What type of work?" I ask suspiciously.

"I need to close a few accounts." He winks, slipping on a black T-shirt before he drops his towel and picks up his black jeans, sliding them up his legs. He pulls on his boots and picks up his phone before he saunters over to where I'm still seated at the counter.

"Have you ever killed anyone you know for money?" I ask.

He doesn't hesitate when he answers, "Yep."

"What if you got a hit on me? Would you do that?"

"It's not so much hits we deal with. We hunt

what others can't find, and we always find what we are after."

"Sounds so scary."

"*I'm* scary."

The doorbell rings again, and he goes to answer it as I mumble, "I've never had this many people come to my door before." I hear Louise's bright, bubbly voice as Zuko lets her in.

I pick up my drink and nod to Louise. "How do you know she won't kill me?" I ask him.

"She won't. I know everything there is to know about her. Even down to her fucking your ex-boss." I choke on my coffee, and Louise's face goes bright red. "It's my job to know things." Then he's out the door without a goodbye, leaving Louise and me staring at each other.

"He—"

"He's a lot," I tell her. "So, about you and Jeff. Care to tell me more?"

"Nope, that's done. Time for me to move on. Oh, what's that?" She catches sight of the dress, and her hands run along the silk skirt exactly as mine did only moments ago. "This is very pretty."

"Thanks. Zuko is taking me to some party or something later."

Her eyes do a quick scan over me. "Let's put curlers in your hair and set them."

"I can do my own hair," I tell her. "Plus, the party isn't until tonight."

"Awesome. A mani-pedi is what we'll do, then. Now, Zuko did say not to leave, but I saw a nail salon just down the road. Think he would mind?" She bites her lip at that question.

"Who cares if he does." I give her an eye roll as I rise from the stool. "Let me get changed real quick. I could use a good pedicure." I go to my room and slip on a maxi dress that hugs my breasts but flows down my body. After sliding on some sandals that will be easy for the pedicure, I walk out to see Louise typing away on her phone.

"Zuko said to stay in the house." She pouts.

"He can go fuck himself." I smile, grabbing my purse. "Let's go." I stroll to the door, but she doesn't follow.

"He won't…you know…hurt me, will he?" she asks worriedly.

"No," I lie.

Well, I hope he won't, but I don't know for sure.

"Okay, good." She grins and jumps up from the couch.

We step outside and decide it's best to walk

down to the salon. Louise fills me on the jobs she's been searching for and skips all the parts about Jeff when I ask her how she's been. I don't push. I wouldn't want to go into detail about fucking someone either if that someone was Jeff.

When we arrive at the salon, we sit down next to each other and are offered drinks. Louise holds up two fingers and tells them two wines. I don't want to tell her that wine doesn't mix well with my medication, but then I realize I never took any today, so it should be fine.

We order more wine and chat about nothing and everything. It's nice to have a girlie conversation. I don't make friends easily because other girls are either intimidated by me or jealous, but Louise is neither.

Just as our nails are drying, the door opens, and in walks Zuko. It's amusing to me how all eyes go to him. He doesn't seem to notice or care though, as he strides straight to where I am seated. He grabs the glass from my hand and pulls it away. His eyes are deadly as he grips hold of the stem, and I swear he is holding it so tightly that any minute it will break away from the glass.

"I thought…" He takes a deep breath. "Are you done?" he asks, clearly unamused and not happy with us. He hasn't even peered at Louise because he's completely fucked off right now.

"Almost. How do my nails look?" I ask him, holding out my hands.

He peers down at them. "Good! Now come on."

I lift my toes. "How do they look?" I say, wiggling them.

"Good enough to eat."

I hear someone sigh at his words but don't check to see who. He pulls out a few hundred-dollar bills and pays the ladies who just did our nails.

"You need to tip," I tell him. He pulls out another hundred and passes it to the lady, who gushes and smiles, thanking him over and over.

"You weren't supposed to drink," he reminds me, handing the glass to the lady, who can't stop saying thank you to him.

"It was only one glass."

"Trouble... I can see the empty glass next to you."

"Okay, it was two. But technically, you took my third." I bite my lip.

He offers me his hand, and I wave at my shoes. He bends and picks them up, sliding them on my feet one at a time, careful not to touch my polish as he does.

"Are you hungry?" he asks.

I look to Louise, who nods her head.

"We're starving. Drinking and self-care can really take a lot out of a woman, you know." I wink and then stand. He holds on to me, making sure a hand is touching me at all times.

Making our way down the street on foot, Louise follows close behind. When we enter a restaurant not too far away, he pulls out my chair, letting me sit, then pulls out the chair for Louise.

"I want a cocktail," I announce.

"No!" He growls out the word succinctly as the waiter arrives at our table. He orders for the whole table, not giving us a chance to check over the menu.

"What if Louise is allergic to what you just ordered?" I sit back in my seat and study him.

"She isn't."

"You can find that information as well?" I ask, amused.

"Yes."

"What have you learned about me?"

"You…" He sits back and eyes me up and

down. "What makes you think I did research on you?"

"Oh, you did. Now, tell me… What did you learn?"

"When you were born, you were born addicted. Your mother was high throughout her pregnancy. She left a note pinned to you that said she couldn't handle your screams, so she dropped you off at a fire station and never looked back. As far as I can tell, she is still high as fuck to this day. And from the age of two, you went from foster home to foster home."

His words jolt me. I don't know anything about my mother. Not even what she looks like. I never really cared to ask or search for her because someone who loves you wouldn't treat you that way. "It's why you don't do drugs, am I correct?"

"Correct," I answer quietly. "Plus, alcohol works just fine for me."

I raise a brow.

"You also like it when I touch you. Any touch of mine…me holding your leg, my hands between your legs—"

"Well, I should go," Louise says, obviously feeling slightly awkward.

"No, stay and eat." I reach for her hand, and she sits back down.

"You also hate to be touched, especially with affection. But not by me."

"Oh, yes, she hates it when I cuddle her, so I make sure to do it every time I see her to get her used to it." Louise laughs.

"You do it on purpose?" I question.

"Of course I do. And because you are the best friend a girl could have. Even if you hate cuddles, I love them, so you *will* take them."

"I'm gonna start kicking you now every time you cuddle me," I threaten, just as the food is placed in front of us.

"You won't. You love me too much."

Damn! She's right. I do.

I look to both of these people who are now fixtures in my life and I wonder how I got here.

I've never had anyone—it's always been me against the world.

But now, I have two people who look after me. Granted, one wants to kill me when he fucks me.

But even then, I keep coming back for more.

THIRTY-ONE

Zuko

"HOW MUCH LONGER IS THIS going to take?" I'm sitting on her bed, watching her while she perches on the floor in front of her full-length mirror doing her makeup. Her hair is already curled and arranged in some half-up half-down style.

Her narrowed eyes meet mine in the reflection of the mirror. "Beauty takes time, Zuko."

"Well, okay then."

"Do you think women just throw together a look and hope for the best? No, we have to shave, wash areas that need to be washed, apply moisturizer everywhere. Dry our hair, style our hair, and hope to God it works. And *then* we do our makeup."

"I've seen you get ready before. You usually

throw things together and hope for the best." I wink and she gasps.

"I look fabulous. But yes, you are correct. On a normal day, I would do that. But for a gala, I want to feel like a princess. Are you denying me that happiness?" she bites back.

Fuck. Okay.

"You know I wouldn't deny you."

"I do not know, hence why I asked." She turns her attention back to her task in hand and continues swiping something on her eyelids. "You do look very handsome, though. Did I tell you that?"

I glance down at my all-black attire. My shirt is silk, and my slacks probably cost more than my watch. But having her compliment them makes me want to go out and buy twenty outfits just like it and wear them every day for her.

"You didn't," I say, hoping how much her words affect me doesn't come through in my voice.

"Well, you do."

I lower to the floor and crawl over to her until I'm at her back. She's wrapped in nothing but a big, fluffy towel. Not able to resist touching her, I place my hand on her bare shoulder and slide my fingers over her smooth skin.

"We can't have sex. That will require me having a shower after, and I can't get my hair wet," she says as my lips touch her neck. She visibly shivers at my kiss, and the brush she was using to apply her makeup pauses an inch away from her face. "Zuko," she says in a breathless whisper. "You don't want me to make you late, and this will definitely make us late."

"Mm-hmm…" is all I can think of as a response.

I reach in front of her and undo the knot in the towel, letting it drop to her lap. I see the top of her ass and am happy to report she is not wearing underwear. When I check over her shoulder into the mirror, I see her eyes darken. She uncrosses her legs, and my eyes pan down her reflection, taking in all of her. And she is beautiful. My hand slides up and grips the back of her neck, pulling her back-ward until she's lying on the floor. I stand, hovering over her, and slide up my sleeves as I stare down at her.

"Zuko…"

"Watch me in the mirror," I demand.

She nods, and I get down on my hands and knees in front of her. She pushes up to her elbows and turns to look at the mirror as my mouth lands on her clit. She jolts a little before she relaxes.

My mouth starts to move, and I push her leg down that's closest to the mirror so she can see from every angle just how much I love tasting her. My tongue works her clit, dipping lower so she can feel it everywhere. When she starts to squirm, I slip a finger inside her, and she pulses around me as I add another, never once slowing my mouth.

"Zuko…" My name comes out on a moan.

"Hmm…" I hum, then ever so slowly swirl my tongue in circles around her clit while she wriggles, screams, and bucks into my mouth.

"Fuck, fuck, fuck," she yells as I feel her come.

"No, it's Zuko, Zuko, Zuko," I correct her, pushing my fingers in deeper. I pull away as she closes her legs around my face, too sensitive now for further touch, and offer her my hand. She takes it, and I help her sit up so she doesn't hurt her belly.

"I—"

"Yes, you can call me God, but I do prefer my name uttered from those lips," I tell her, rubbing them with the fingers that were just inside of her. She opens her mouth, and I lean forward and kiss her. She groans as I palm one of her breasts, squeezing her nipple. I pull back, and she graces me with a slow smile.

"You need to get ready." I stand, and she turns back to the mirror, leaving her towel where it is. When I look down at her, I see her swollen lips— not the ones I just kissed, the ones I tasted.

"Can you grab my dress from the closet?" she asks as she resumes applying her makeup. "Or would you prefer my lips to go around your cock before I put on lipstick?" She raises a brow.

"I'll wait until after. I'd rather you stain my cock with those luscious lips." She grins, happy with my response, as I retrieve her dress. She applies her lip gloss and then stands. I unzip the dress, and she steps into it, shimmying it up her waist, then slides her arms into the lace sleeves before turning around for me to zip it up.

"Is black the theme for tonight?" she asks.

"Yes."

"It must be one of your parties, for sure." She giggles.

"It is my party," I inform her.

Her eyes go wide. "What? Is it really?"

"Yes. It was my idea when I was first introduced into this world to meet those who would likely one day be my competition. But what it turned out to be was a way to make contacts. When they can't do the job, they come to me."

She shakes her head.

"Um... Wow, okay." Grabbing her sky-high heels from the floor at the foot of the bed, I kneel down and slide them on for her, so she doesn't have to bend.

"Do you plan to wear any panties?"

"Nope." She smiles happily. "Will that be an issue?"

"Well, as long as no one else knows, I don't see an issue." I shrug.

"Good, because I wasn't going to wear any even if it was." She turns, grabs her purse, and heads to her bedroom door.

"Do you plan to eventually get your own place?" she asks.

"Why? Do you want me gone already, even after I just made you come?" I question.

She shrugs. "I don't much like sharing."

"I sleep on the couch," I remind her.

"No, you don't. You come in and hold me."

She's right, but I won't confirm that.

"Do you not sleep better when I'm there?"

"I do," she answers quietly over her shoulder as she leaves the room.

———

"Just stay by my side," I tell Alaska as I reach for her hand.

She doesn't pull away as I slide mine into hers.

Her eyes scan the crowd, her face half hidden by a lacy, black mask that matches her dress. I pull on my mask and wonder why I came up with this stupid idea years ago. I see a few people I know—dirty, scumbag killers—and think how much I hate most of the men here. Some come into this life because they have no other option, and some do it for the love of killing. I'm a little of both. I fell into it, but I never let it turn me the way some of the people here have been turned.

"Zuko, you brought a date," Pops says, coming up to stand near us. He glances at Alaska and then back to me. "You never bring a date."

"Hello, Michelle." I nod to Pop's new plaything. She inclines her head back to me but quickly avoids eye contact. Alaska looks around, not paying us any attention.

The room is somewhat dark. Two waiters move through the crowd, and even they are people who are just getting started in this world.

They want to be like us.

They want our secrets.

They want to be me.

Someone clinks a glass, and the twenty or so people who are here move toward the table. I spot my brothers at the head of the table where I usually sit with them, but tonight I sit to the side next to Alaska. When my brothers see her, Kyson scowls, and Kenzo gives her a head nod.

"You brought a date?" Mario asks. He's known for killing prostitutes—hired by the men who fucked them.

He's a dick as well.

"So unlike you." He turns to Alaska and offers his hand. She doesn't take it, instead sitting down in the seat I pulled out for her—right next to Kyson, with me on her other side. He grumbles something under his breath, and it makes her laugh.

I love that fucking sound.

Almost as much as I love her.

THIRTY-TWO

Alaska

ZUKO IS TENSE TONIGHT.

He's always got an edgy feel about him, but not like this.

It's like he doesn't want to be here.

"We don't bring dates," Kyson grumbles.

"I could be your date too, if you want." I wink at him.

"Like hell. You are a crazy bitch." He shakes his head.

"Your ability to antagonize Kyson is my favorite of your traits, Alaska," Kenzo interjects.

Food is placed down at the center of the long table for us to serve ourselves. Once the waiters are gone, the chatter around the table resumes.

"So it's not my good looks? Or the way I make your brother stalk me without my permission?" I ask Kenzo with my head tilted to the side innocently.

Everyone has some type of mask on, but even with that, I feel a few eyes on me.

"Zuko."

I turn back to the table to search for the person who called Zuko's name. Zuko is facing the end of the table where a few men sit talking to each other in hushed tones.

"Yes?"

"Is she an offering?" one asks, nodding at me.

Zuko straightens next to me. "Excuse me?" he growls, a threat evident in his tone.

"Why else would you bring her here dressed like that? To not only tease but to give as well?"

"She is my date. Just as you are all welcome to bring one."

"Pops is the only one stupid enough to bring a date," one of the men says.

The room falls deadly silent.

"Yeah, Pops. Do you tell Zuko here what we do with your dates?" someone else adds.

My eyes fly up to the lady with Pops. She isn't the same one from the boys' birthday party. She looks down to her lap and says nothing. I glance over at Pops to see him watching Zuko.

"What do you do with them?" Zuko asks.

"They do what any of the men want," Pops answers.

"You pay them?" Zuko questions.

Pops ghosts the back of his hand over her chest, and she visibly flinches.

"No, they do it for protection. Isn't that right, sweetheart?" He squeezes her shoulder.

"Seems she doesn't want you touching her," I can't help blurting out.

If you dropped a pin right now, you would hear it.

That's how silent the room is.

I glance back at the woman to see her staring at me with her eyes wide. I turn to Pops and see contempt written all over his face.

"I'd watch your words, whore, or you will end up just like her... Needing my protection."

Zuko goes to stand, but I quickly place my hand on his thigh, halting him. Pops notices, and it seems to make him smile.

"I want that whore. I bet I can teach her a thing or two. One being how to speak to a man," a balding asshole halfway down the table says as he leers at me.

Someone slams their fist on the table, and we all turn to see Kyson fuming. "Shut the fuck up, all of you. I want to eat already," he bellows.

A few laugh at his outburst, and I let go of Zuko's thigh and pick up my fork. I hear the other men still talking about me and how they plan to fuck me.

Zuko is as still as a statue.

When he stands, a few quiet, but they go back to talking as he steps behind his brothers and stands between them. He leans down to speak, and when I peek up, I see Pops glaring at me.

"So, what do you charge?" the man who was sitting on the other side of Zuko asks me. "I can afford it. You seem like expensive pussy."

"You kill prostitutes," Kyson mumbles, and I straighten at his words.

"So? She seems like the expensive type, and I only kill the trashy ones..." he pauses before he adds with a sinister smile, "sometimes." He pulls away as someone else says something I don't quite hear, but Zuko seems to have. He moves in a flash, pulling the mask from his face and stalking toward the men at the end of the table. I push my seat back and stop him.

"Can you escort me to the bathroom?" I ask, offering him my hand. He pauses and looks down at it. He crushes his mask in his fist but takes my hand. Making our way out of the room, conversations continue behind us, but no one says anything loud enough for us to hear. As soon as we get to the bathroom, I go into the stall and close the door while he leans against the counter.

"Don't let them get to you," I tell him.

"It's not me they're talking about. It's you," he replies. "Words hardly affect me. They could call me the worst asshole to grace this earth, and I wouldn't care."

I pull open the door and see him watching me. After I wash my hands, I then step in front of him, put my arms around his waist, and lean into him. "So why are you mad? I can feel you are." I bury my nose in his neck, breathing in his scent. He smells expensive. And delicious.

"They don't have permission to speak about you *in any manner*."

"It doesn't bother me." He wraps both arms around me and kisses the top of my head.

"I could…help you forget," I coo, my hand

sliding between us. As I palm his cock through his pants, it jolts.

"I would never turn you down, but tonight I have to." He steps back, but before he gets too far, he leans in and kisses me on the lips, stealing my breath away. When he pulls away, he lingers. "I think I'm falling in love with you." His words make my heart skip a beat, and he doesn't wait for me to respond before he grabs my hand and leads me back to the room. He pulls my seat out when we get to the now quiet table and sits next to me.

"I really want to fuck that whore, Zuko. Seriously, how much for her? If you don't share, I'll find her and fuck her anyway."

Zuko's eyes lock on mine at the man's taunt.

Some of the others laugh, agreeing with him, before he smiles at me and says, "Cover your ears, Trouble."

He waits for me to just do that. And then I sit there, shocked, as he lifts a gun and, without warning or moving from his seat, shoots the man next to him in the head, then goes around the table until each and every man is dead, leaving only his brothers, Pops, and Pop's "date."

He pauses his shooting spree with the gun aimed at Pops, who is smiling like he is happy with what Zuko has just done. We're all covered in blood, and the food is now inedible, and he still hasn't lowered the gun.

The woman next to Pops is screaming, and she can't seem to shut up. Kenzo is closer to her, so he leans over, and whacks her over the back of the head. She falls face-first into her plate of food. I sit there, stunned, not sure how we got to this point.

"You wouldn't shoot me, Zuko. I'm the only father figure you know. You would kill me over a girl?"

That seems to make Zuko madder as his finger tightens on the trigger.

I can't move.

It's like my hands are glued to my ears.

And now I understand why he wears black.

"You better apologize to Alaska right the fuck now. And if you think you can get away with mistreating her again, then think again," Zuko warns.

"Yeah, bastard gave me a black eye over her," Kyson grumbles, grinning. "He will for sure kill you over her." He chuckles.

Pops seems to finally understand what's happening.

"You don't even know her," Pops argues.

"I know her well enough," Zuko replies. "Apologize. This is your only chance."

Pops glares at me and grinds his jaw before he says, "I'm sorry. I won't talk in that manner to you again."

I don't respond.

I think a part of me is frozen on the spot.

I knew Zuko was a little crazy. I mean, I'm not dumb. But holy shit.

"Trouble…" He hands the gun to Kenzo. Kenzo takes it and slides it into his waistband.

"Is that why you didn't want head? You didn't want me to see the gun?" I ask him stunned and my mind going completely blank from what just happened, referring to our moment in the bathroom, but a small part of me is wondering if he really said no earlier because he was hiding his gun from me.

Someone coughs, and someone sounds like they are choking as he reaches for me and pulls my hands down from my head.

"Yes, you would have freaked."

"You've done worse to me with a knife," I remind him.

He smirks and cups my face. "Ready to go home?"

"Home," I say, and he stands, offering me his hand again. I take it. And I wonder if I will take it for the rest of my life. I keep on taking his hand, even knowing who he is, and I wonder why.

"Oh, don't worry. You know we'll clean up your mess," Kyson says sarcastically.

"I already ordered the cleaners," Zuko replies as the doors open, and men enter dressed in hazard suits with gurneys. "I'm taking Alaska home."

I offer a small wave, unsure of what else to do, and walk out, not looking back.

As soon as we're in the car, he drives off.

A few miles down the road, he pulls up to a drive-thru and orders us two burgers with fries. My mouth starts to water as soon as I smell the food.

"You didn't eat," he says, passing me the food. I grab out my burger, then unwrap his, handing it to him as he drives.

"Neither did you."

"I'm sorry about the dress," he tells me before biting into his burger.

I get a warm feeling in my chest, thinking about those lips and that mouth, and about how only hours earlier they were bringing me pleasure.

And then those words.

He thinks he loves me.

Sure, men have said, *"oh God, I love you,"* as we fuck. But the words held no weight when they said them. The words never had true meaning until tonight.

Until him.

"I can wash it."

"No, it will have to be destroyed," he states. "But I'll buy you a new one."

"Good."

I take a bite of my burger as we pull up to my place. We sit in the car and eat in silence until we're both full.

When we're done, I turn to face him.

"I don't think anyone around you likes me," I say nervously.

"That doesn't matter."

"But it does. They are your family," I push.

"Kenzo likes you, and Kyson is warming up to you. You hurt his ego, is all."

"And Pops?"

"It doesn't matter if he likes you. He knows where I stand now, and I will not have anyone insult you. I'll happily show him how to appreciate you by taking a knife to his neck."

"So violent," I whisper.

"For you." He leans in and grabs the back of

my head, pulling me in for a kiss. He kisses me on the lips and smiles against them. "You taste like hamburger…" he kisses me again, "and all the things I want in this life."

I can't help but smile.

I never knew I wanted someone in my life the way he has inserted himself into it, until he did. Granted, our relationship has been rocky. But I think all the best ones start out that way.

We finally get out and head into the apartment.

My phone rings, and I answer it without a second thought as I enter the bedroom and hear the shower turn on.

"You've reached Sage from You Beat It, We Spit It. First, let's start with your name." I step out of the bedroom so he can't hear me. I open the apartment door and stand in the hallway as I wait for the person to speak.

"Hello, Trouble…" I drop the phone and turn back to see Zuko, shirtless, holding his phone to his ear as he leans against the doorjamb. "Seems you have been hiding something from me."

I smile at him.

And then I turn on my heel and run.

THIRTY-THREE

Zuko

AS THE SKIRT of her black dress fans out behind her, I keep watching.

I'm impressed by how fast those legs can go considering she has those sky-high heels on. Pocketing my phone, I chase after her. She's fast, but I'm a hell of a lot faster. Catching up to her, I wrap my arm around her being careful not to touch her midsection in case I hurt her.

She yelps but stops.

"Why did you run, Trouble?" She is breathing heavily and locks eyes with me. "Are you scared?"

"No," she states.

And I believe her.

"How long have you known it was me?" I ask.

"Every time I called, I mentioned the other woman. When did you figure it out?"

"In the bar, that first night when you walked up to me to save me from that dude."

"I heard you speak that night, and when I asked for your name, and you told me it was, Alaska I thought I must've been mistaken. But then…" I reach for her and pick her up bridal style and carry her back to her place.

"But then?" she asks, her eyes on me as I walk. "When did you work out it was me?"

"When I stayed here the first night and your phone wouldn't shut up."

Oh, shit.

"Do you need money? Is that why you do it?"

"I always need money. I'm going to hustle for money until the day I die," she answers truthfully. "It's what you do when you go from never having any to finally finding some. You never want it to go away again."

"You can have what I have," I offer, meaning every single word.

"You have nothing. I burned your house down," she reminds me.

I kick her front door open and stroll inside. Striding into the bathroom with her still in my arms, I carefully set her down before my hands lift to unzip her dress.

"I have four other houses, two apartments, and one hotel chain," I inform her, and her head swivels around to face me. "In fact, you stayed in one of my hotels. Why do you think the doorman didn't call the police on me? It's because I pay his wage."

"Holy shit!" She breathes out as her dress drops to the floor. I turn the shower on, and she steps in. I pick up her dress and my bloody shirt and strip off my pants. Then I carry them out and place them in a plastic bag. They will need to be burned, but that's a tomorrow job.

When I go back into the bathroom, she's already done cleaning up. So I step into the shower and wash myself as she ties her hair up for the night. She takes one last look at me before she walks out. I turn the water off, step onto the bath mat, and dry myself off. By the time I enter the bedroom, she's already half asleep. I take a few moments to gaze at her perfection before turning to head to the couch. But before I get through the door, she calls my name.

"I might have nightmares tonight," she whispers.

And she doesn't have to ask me twice.

I round the bed and climb in, pulling her to me.

I wrap my arm tight around her, and before long, she's asleep.

With no nightmares.

———

"Pops is mad," Kyson says, kicking a can. He came over to meet me for my morning run.

"That's none of my business. He can either fuck off and leave me alone or deal with it."

He turns to face me. "You have never turned against him before. He's confused."

"There has never been a *her* before."

"So you love her?" he asks, surprised. "She isn't a phase?"

"She is not. I would take your life if you hurt her."

He scrunches his forehead in thought and looks away.

We start running again until we near her apartment. She was sound asleep when I left and probably will be when I return.

"I have news," he announces.

I stop and face him.

"Lilly's getting married and sent me an invite." He pulls out the crumpled paper from his pocket.

I'm surprised my brother is bringing her up but I don't let my expression show that. "You said you didn't love her," I remind him. "So what does it matter?"

"I said I didn't know if I did." I take the invitation from him and check the date.

"The wedding is in a week."

"I've had the invitation for months," he confesses. "I think I'm going to go," he adds.

"That would be a mistake," I state. "You should *not* go to her wedding. You let her go. And now she is marrying someone else."

His hand lifts, and he scratches the back of his head.

"What if I want her back?"

I inhale a deep breath.

Lilly loved Kyson more than he could ever love her. If he ever did, that is.

"Is this why you wanted out?" I ask.

"No. Yes. Maybe." He sighs. "I just thought... I want what you have right now. I know most men like us don't. But this life is lonely, and I want to share it with someone. It's hard to do that in this life though." He isn't wrong. It takes someone extremely special or fucked-up to agree to this lifestyle.

We are all fucked-up in more ways than one.

"Do you still want to leave? If you do, you know I will support you."

He smiles, lifts his hand, and smacks my arm.

"Look…she's making you soft already." He laughs.

"No, she isn't. But you are in this life because of me. I am a lifer and there is no way I will ever leave. It's what I know. And it may be what you know, but you *can* leave, Kyson."

He seems to process what I'm saying.

"I'll sort it out."

"Have you told Kenzo?" I ask.

"No, Kenzo is like you… A lifer."

He is. Kenzo and I are different from Kyson. Kyson shows more…feelings, I guess I would say. Kenzo and I prefer to be silent. It's safer that way.

Not that Kyson isn't as deadly as Kenzo.

They are different—no matter that they are twins.

"I still don't think you should go to her wedding," I say again.

"Whose wedding?" Alaska asks from the door. "I love weddings." She grins.

"Be my plus one," Kyson says.

I told her Kyson was warming up to her.

"Ha, that's a no. You *will* take her to make Lilly jealous, and that would mean you are touching Alaska. That is not going to happen," I add, walking inside.

Kyson follows, not even caring that it's not my house. "Come on, let me take her," he begs.

"Nope," I reply, parking myself at the stove to start cooking breakfast. Kyson sits at the breakfast bar next to Alaska.

"Shouldn't this be my choice?" Alaska asks.

"Nope," he and I say in unison.

She crosses her arms over her chest. "Why not?"

"Because it's not you that he'll hit. It'll be me," Kyson replies.

"Oh…" Alaska says.

"Yeah." Kyson looks back at me. "How long do you plan to stay here? It's too far for runs."

"You ran here?" Alaska asks, surprised.

"I did. We always run."

"Maybe I should start running," she muses. "Nah, fuck that. Too much effort."

Kyson laughs at her response.

"Yeah, you should run, just not with us." He

winks at her before he looks back at me. "What do I do?"

I dish up the food and give a plate to each of them.

"About the wedding?" Alaska asks.

"You just want to fuck her again, at her wedding, of all places," I say.

Kyson smirks, and I know it's the truth.

"Oh Lord… I am so not going to that as your date, then," Alaska adds.

"You wouldn't be his date." I growl.

"I can find you someone, if that's what you want," Alaska offers.

"Nope," Kyson says, shoving his mouth full of food. "I'll find my own date to make her jealous. Then I'll fuck her in her wedding dress so she remembers me forever." He winks at Alaska.

I shake my head as I eat my food.

Alaska stands and turns to me. "I need help picking an outfit," she says.

I stand tall, ignoring my food as I study her. "What for?" I question.

"A new job. I need to find work, and I applied for a few jobs and got an interview."

"I'm sure you can go back to the bar," Kyson interjects.

"Nope, never want to go back there again." She turns toward her room and peers over her shoulder. "Are you coming, or am I getting naked by myself?"

"Kyson, get the fuck out and lock the door as you leave," I bark out. I wipe my hands on my basketball shorts and follow her into the bedroom.

Alaska pulls up her shirt, leaving her standing there gloriously naked.

I hear the front door close as she lays back on the bed.

"I hope you don't mind my little fib. I mean I do need help picking an outfit but right now I'm ready for you to play again, but with your hands, Zuko. No knife or bag. Do you understand?"

I nod my head as I make my way to the shower.

I hear her voice follow me, calling, "Where are you going?"

After stripping off my clothes I move straight under the spray. Quickly washing my body, I turn to see her leaning against the counter, naked and smiling.

"I was sweaty, and I can't contaminate you. You are simply too stunning for that." She blushes, and it makes my cock hard. She notices, her eyes falling to my erection.

I turn the water off and step out. Securing a

towel around my waist, I cup her chin in my hand and ask, "Are you sure?" I don't want her to be nervous or have any regrets about our sex life.

"You'll stop when I say stop?" she questions.

"Of course I will," I whisper, leaning in and kissing her lips. Kissing them once, twice, and a third time just to be sure. I pull back and smile.

"No knives," she reiterates.

"Not until you ask."

She huffs a laugh. "Yeah, that's never going to happen."

I don't reply as we make our way back to the bedroom. She sits on the edge of the bed, and I stand between her legs. Lifting her chin with a finger, I gaze down at her.

"I've never wanted to fuck someone so much in my life."

Her hand raises and wraps around my cock.

Gripping it tightly, she smirks. "How bad?" Her voice is like silk.

"Are you Sage or Alaska right now?" Because that voice is how she spoke to me on the phone.

"Which one do you prefer?" she purrs.

"You. I want *you*."

She gives my cock a squeeze.

"Both are me." She leans forward, and her lips

touch my cock. "Sage wants you to let her taste. Alaska wants you to fuck her." I growl as her mouth envelops me. She is stunning with her lips stretched wide around my cock. I'm careful not to slam her head down my length because she is still healing, and I have to be mindful of that.

Mindful of *her*.

Her mouth works me over perfectly, and she grabs my balls and rolls them in her hand.

Fuck.

How is she so perfect for me?

How did I get so lucky?

Pulling back, she wipes her mouth as I stare down at her. She peeks back at me, with her lavender hair in a messy bun on top of her head.

I step back so she can't reach me again. "All in due time, Trouble. It's best you lie down, so you don't hurt yourself." I smile.

Her eyes go wide for a second before she does as I ask.

Now it's time to play.

With my favorite toy to ever grace this earth.

Oh, what fun we will have.

THIRTY-FOUR

Alaska
_____

HE DISPLAYS moments of malevolence but also moments of tenderness. Then there are moments of complete consumption of me. And I want him to consume me. I almost want to beg for it, despite my pride telling me never to beg a man.

I guess that's where it would be different with us.

He doesn't make me feel like I would have to or that I would feel less than by doing so.

He hovers above me, his hands lightly feathering my body, causing goose bumps to break out over my skin. I gasp as he reaches my nipples, his mouth closing around the hard peak and sucking before I feel his teeth bite into it. He repeats the pattern with the other breast, his cock teasing my entrance as he touches me.

I can feel myself getting wetter and wetter at his touch.

He is careful not to put his weight on me or touch my stomach, but right now, I don't care. It doesn't even hurt that much anymore.

Or maybe it's just the endorphins kicking in.

Either way, I am lost to it.

Lost to *him*.

And what an amazing way to be lost.

He crawls farther down my body, his mouth gliding along my skin. I lift my hands to my hair, gripping, then sliding my fingers through it as his mouth lands on my pussy. I hear his intake of breath before his tongue slides between my lips and he licks me.

It's heaven, and I buck my hips at his touch.

Fuck.

His touch is amazing.

His mouth leaves me, and I glance down to see him smirking, his eyes intently watching me.

"You look fucking beautiful when you want my cock." Zuko lowers his head back between my legs and pushes himself closer to me, teasing me as he hovers above me. "Is she needy?" he asks.

I can only nod my head.

He pushes closer, just the tip, before he grabs my hands and places them at my sides. "Keep them still, do you understand?" I nod again, all words lost to me, as his hands come up and caress my neck. He places his thumbs on either side of my throat, and then he slowly inserts himself into me. I feel something, and when I check, I see he's wearing a cock ring—one made to please us both. It rubs my clit as he pushes in, and I flinch, but he holds me down, my hands remain at my sides.

His mouth comes down on mine as he starts a slow rhythm, the cock ring moving and gliding along my clit with a slight vibration.

Shit! That feels good.

I feel myself getting there already. *How can he do that so fast?* I try to stay still, as he requested, but the pressure is becoming too much. It's all too much. I try not to buck my hips, but then his hands tighten slightly on my neck. He leans down and kisses me as he increases the pressure further, still thrusting into me.

I lift my hand and grip his, but he doesn't release me, just keeps on thrusting and applying pressure until my head feels light, my body feels high, and I can't contain it. I squeeze his hands tighter, and he eases the pressure a fraction, and when I suck in a breath, he slams into me, and I feel everything *all at once.*

My body comes alive.

An orgasm I didn't even feel building hits me hard—harder than anything before it.

A scream rips from my throat.

Zuko crashes his lips to mine and kisses me again.

The speed of his thrusts increases, and that ring is still vibrating on my clit.

"I—"

"Come again, Trouble," he orders, gripping one of my thighs.

I'm not sure how I can, but he doesn't stop. He pulls out, looks between us, and slaps my clit, hard. I scream again, and he pushes ever so slowly back into me. I watch as he sucks one of his fingers and then places it on my clit.

Holy shit.

His cock is hitting that spot inside me.

His hand and the vibration are taking over.

I can't hold on any longer as I feel my body go so high, my breathing pauses, and I have to remember to inhale and exhale.

I need to breathe.

"That was hot!" Zuko pants, wiping the hair that has fallen out from my bun away from my face. "I could do that again." I look up to him and have to remember to breathe. Is this what relationships are like. Is this what I have been missing out on?

"Well, I need a break." I smile up at him.

He pulls out and lies next to me and I turn to my side and study him.

"What?" he asks, staring at the ceiling.

"Did that satisfy you? I mean...sexually? Did it get you off?" I ask.

His head shifts on the pillow until his eyes meet mine. "The sight of you gets me off. Why would you ask that?"

"I know you like it..." I say it nervously, "rougher."

He smirks, reaches for my tit, and pinches my nipple. "We can work you up to that in due time."

"What if I don't want to? What if that is my limit?" I bite my lip as I wait for his answer.

"Then that will be fine," he says matter-of-factly.

"But you like that shit," I insist.

"I like *you*. Would I prefer to fuck you like my good little whore? Yes and no. I'm honestly just happy to fuck you. To have you. Do I want to hurt you? No."

"But you did hurt me," I tell him.

"No, I scared you. There is a difference. You came, or did you forget?"

I know he's right. But still.

His phone rings, and he groans as he sits up and reaches for it on his side of the bed.

His. Ha. Never thought I would think that.

"I'll be there." Zuko hangs up, stands, and grabs some clothes.

"Where are you going?" I ask as I pull a sheet over my still-naked body. I watch as he pulls off the cock ring, and I smile at that movement.

"Stop looking at me like that or I won't be able to leave."

I smile even wider. He groans and continues getting dressed. "I'm going to see Pops," he adds.

"Can I come?" I ask, sitting up.

"Are you sure you want to?"

"He's your family, and I think I should try to get along with him." I rise from the bed and pull some clothes out of a drawer, then go into the bathroom. I use the toilet first and wipe before I dress. When I'm ready, I find him waiting at the door with my phone and bag in hand. I lean up and kiss his cheek, and he grabs my ass in return.

"You know I'm not moving out, right?" he says, closing the door. "Since you burned my house down and all." I can't help the laugh that bubbles up in me. As soon as we get to his car, I freeze. Standing next to it is Sarah with her arms crossed over her chest. She spots me and smiles, but when she sees Zuko, her smile dies.

"I came to apologize," she whispers.

Neither of us say anything for a while as she stares at the sidewalk but then her eyes find mine. "I didn't…" Zuko moves in close to me and Sarah raises her hands.

"Jeff always pitted us against one another, told me you were his main girl. Then he would fuck me and tell me how amazing you are. It made me hate you even more," she admits dropping her arms to her sides. "Anyway, I'm leaving. Going to Europe and hope never to return. I just wanted to say sorry."

I remain silent.

She waits for me to reply, but I have no words for her.

I hate the bitch.

It was her choice to be a cunt, not mine.

She hated me from the moment she met me, and so now I don't care what she has to say.

Zuko leads me to his car and opens the door. Sarah watches, still waiting. When I get in, and he shuts the door, he walks around to the driver's side, says something to her, then climbs behind the wheel.

"What did you say?" I ask.

"That she better run far away," he answers without hesitation.

With a deep sigh, I reach for his hand and hold it in mine. We stay that way the whole drive to Pop's, and when we arrive, we stroll to the door hand in hand. Pops opens the door and gazes down at our hands, then at me, before his eyes lock on Zuko.

"You brought company?" he asks.

"Yes. Do you intend to let us in?"

After a beat, Pops steps aside and lets us in.

"Maybe she can go outside with the girls while we talk," Pops suggests.

"Or not," Zuko counters, not letting go of my hand.

Pop's jaw twitches at his words.

We follow him into his office and Pops sits

behind his desk. His large leather chair does nothing to diminish his imposing frame.

"Kyson wants to leave," Pops states. I stand there, not sure what to say or if I should say anything. "Did you know?"

"Has he told you this?" Zuko asks.

Pops shakes his head. "No, he was mumbling, and I overheard him talking to Kenzo."

"Let him be, then," Zuko tells him.

Just then, Pop's girlfriend—*plaything, maybe*—walks in, holding a glass of wine. She smiles as she approaches.

"Zuko, you brought your sweet friend again. It's so nice to see you," she greets.

"If you call burning a house down sweet, I'm sure that's what she is." Zuko smiles.

I cough and cover my mouth.

"She what?" Pops asks, incredulous.

I step away from Zuko, who gives me a playful look. "So, what are you drinking?" I ask Pop's girlfriend. It's a terrible attempt to change the subject and everyone knows it.

"You sure are smiling a lot more," Pops says. I hear him even though he tried to say it low enough for only Zuko to hear.

"That's what she does to me," Zuko replies.

"Do you plan to quit as well?" Pops asks.

"You know this is my life. And she is part of it now. But if she asked me to leave, I would. But don't stress over it. She accepts me."

"Good…good," Pops replies, but I can hear the uncertainty in his voice.

The door opens, and Kenzo enters. Zuko moves over to talk to him, and Pops turns to face me.

"You do know what you're in for, right?" he asks, low enough that Zuko can't hear.

"And what's that?"

"Zuko is a cold-blooded killer. He is the best at what he does. I've never seen anyone like him in my life. He is so good that I dropped every other person I was training and working with to have him to myself," he confesses. "His brothers are just as spectacular."

"Do you see me as a threat?" I question.

"I see you as his, and that's as far as I want to see you, to be honest. I don't want a problem with you, Alaska. I will respect his wishes to be with you, and leave you alone, because I respect him. But if you fuck him over—"

"You'll what?" Zuko says, coming up behind him.

"There is nothing I wouldn't do for you," Pops says, turning around and nodding to Kenzo.

"It's fine. Pops and I have an understanding. We're all good," I assure Zuko, taking his hand and lacing our fingers together. He squeezes mine, knowing that I'm simply letting this all be. I don't want to ruin what they call 'family.' That's the last thing I want to do.

"Good, now let's cook. Barbecue time," Kyson says, coming through the door.

When did he arrive? All eyes turn to him. He smiles at everyone and flips me off, so I flip him off in return.

"I can still find you a date," I offer.

"Fuck off," he grumbles, and I can't help but laugh.

Everyone starts making their way outside, but Zuko holds me back and turns me around so I'm facing him.

"Do you love me?" he asks.

"Do you want the truth?" He sucks in a breath and nods once. "Yes. Head-over-heels, would-let-you-strangle-me-again kind of love. But definitely not fuck-me-with-a-knife love."

Someone coughs behind me and laughs, so I flip

my finger back to him, knowing it's Kyson. "Damn, brother."

Zuko pays him no attention, keeping his eyes on me.

"So, I can move in?" he asks.

"You told me you already were," I remind him.

"Yeah, I was going to regardless." I wrap my arms around his back and hold him to me. "For someone who hates touch, you sure do crave mine."

I lean up and whisper, "About as much as I crave your cock." He picks me up, and my legs instantly wrap around his waist like they are jigsaw pieces that have found their home around his body.

"We can always fix that craving," he says as he carries me to the bathroom and then has his way with me.

Best sex.

Every time with him.

I'm completely consumed by him.

The bad.

The good.

But most of all the evil.

Epilogue

Alaska

"I..." I can't even finish my thought as Zuko stalks toward me.

It's been a few months since we started living together. And to say it's been going well would be an understatement.

It's been amazing.

When I can't sleep, he is there to help calm me.

When I need him for anything, he is always there.

I couldn't have asked for a better man to be my person if I tried.

And that's saying a lot considering how determined I was to stay single.

"Why are you naked?" I ask.

"My clothes were covered in blood," he replies casually.

"But you showered," I point out.

It's not that I don't enjoy seeing him naked—it's always an incredibly delicious sight. But Louise is about to come over as she wants to share some news with me that she, for some reason, couldn't tell me over the phone.

"Does my cock offend you?" he jokes, thrusting his hips and making me laugh as it bobs up and down.

"No, it usually pleases me very much," I state, smiling.

"Usually?" he questions, his eyes turning to slits as he frowns.

"Yes, *usually*. Sometimes when I see it, it's in the shower, so then it clearly isn't pleasing me because it's not touching me."

"You look real good in that dress," he croons, coming closer and gripping my hips. I fall into his embrace and feel him harden further.

"I wore it to work."

"Hmm… I wonder what it would look like if…"

He spins me and grabs my hair, pushing me face-down, so my ass is in his crotch, and I'm bent over with my head down near my knees. A knock sounds on the door as he pulls at my hair, but he doesn't let me back up. "I reckon I can make you come while she knocks on that door." He pushes harder into me, and I yelp in pleasure.

"I…" I lose words when it comes to him.

This man? He leaves me speechless.

Some may call me crazy for loving Zuko, but I don't know how to stop loving him.

"That's right, Trouble. You know you want it."

Louise knocks again. He pulls up my dress and slaps my ass. I am wearing a G-string, and he slides it to the side. Then I feel him at my entrance, playing and teasing me there. Not quite entering me but rubbing against all the most sensitive parts of me. His grip on my hair tightens, and he pulls a little harder.

Since the night I agreed to let him live here—because I burned his house down—we have played and played some more. The knife thing I haven't quite warmed up to yet, and I'm not sure I ever will. He does love that knife though, about as much as he loves me I would say. He always carries it with him. Unless he's in this house, then it's put away.

When it comes to choking? Well, that I love. It puts me right on the edge and leaves me wanting more. It makes him happy, which in turn, makes me even happier. Zuko is a different ball game from what I am used to in men.

He doesn't want.

He simply needs me.

And that's it.

"Zuko…" I whisper.

"Yes, Trouble?"

"If you don't enter me—" He slides straight in as Louise knocks again, and I have the wind knocked clean out of my lungs.

Once I have my equilibrium back, I murmur-yell to Louise, "Just getting dressed. Can you give me second!" Then I slap my hand over my mouth as he pushes in harder, and pulls back out, slamming in and out of me in a slow but tender punishment. He reaches around and places his fingers on my clit, rubbing in slow circles. Then, just as he pulls all the way out of me, he slaps my pussy, lets me go, and steps back. I stand there, my eyes wide, as I watch him walk out of the room.

"You asshole!" I scream.

"I'll give you guys a minute," I hear Louise say from the other side of the door.

I grunt and pull my panties down my legs and then follow him to the bedroom. I find him looking through the closet for clothes. I grab his arm, turning him around. Zuko smiles, knowing I'm madder than hell, and my indignation is showing heavily on my face, but he can't deny he didn't finish either.

He's still hard.

Incredibly hard.

"Why didn't you finish us off?" I push him, and he takes a step backward.

"Your friend is here." He smirks, knowing full well what he's doing.

"Get on the floor, now."

He does as I say and sits down. I place a foot on either side of him and push him back until he's lying on the floor, then I reach between us, grab his cock, and put it at my entrance. "Actually, maybe I should finish without you," I say, going to stand, but he grabs me so I can't move.

"That's not an option." He slides his hand between us and rubs my clit. "This wants me. Now, sit." I do as he says and slowly lower myself on him.

I hear Louise knock again, but I'm now fully seated on his cock, and what a beautiful cock it is. My hips move back and forth, back and forth, getting all the friction I need knowing an explosion is imminent.

His hands grip my hips before one makes its way up to my neck and pulls me down, so our lips smash together. The hand around my throat squeezes, and I feel myself building and building.

Only he can make me come this hard.

And this fast.

It's like he has a magic cock.

As soon as I come, I feel him do the same.

His hand tightens around my windpipe, and I start to become lightheaded. He releases me before I pass out and then smiles.

"You better let your friend in." He pulls me back in for one last kiss before he stands with him still inside me. When he's upright, he lifts me up and then places my feet on the floor. "I'll just take another shower." He winks before he disappears.

Shaking my head, I walk out and pull the door open.

Louise is standing there, biting her nails. When she finally sees me, relief washes over her face, and she blurts out, "I'm pregnant. And it's Jeff's." Her face pales as my eyes go wide in shock. "And so is Sarah," she adds.

"Holy. Shit," are the only words I can seem to make come out of my mouth.

"Yeah. What am I going to do?"

"Take him for all his money." I laugh, only half joking. "Do you want to keep the baby?" I know it's not a question most people want to hear. But it's reality in some people's lives, and who am I to judge their life choices?

"I don't know." I lead her inside, and she sits next to me on the couch. "I don't want Jeff. I am over that man. But I'm so unsure."

"You can always raise the baby yourself," I suggest.

"I don't know if I can do that either."

"We can help." I touch her leg, and she glances up at me, smiling.

"That's a no," Zuko says as he enters the room, and I roll my eyes.

"He will. I can butter him up and make him say yes to anything. Power of the pussy and all." I wink, and Louise can't help but laugh.

"I'm leaving. Goodbye, Trouble." Zuko kisses the top of my head before he heads out the door.

"You two are so lucky," Louise gushes.

Ha! If only she knew how hard it was to get to this place in our lives.

How hard it can be some days.

Not because of anything Zuko does wrong. But it's all about me realizing it's okay to be loved and to want love in return.

It's a battle I didn't know I had to fight.

It's a battle I know I need to win.

And I will fight the battle every day if it involves Zuko.

"One day, I want someone to love me the way he loves you."

"You'll have that," I tell her. "It's just a matter of time."

"I hope so." She smiles. "I think I'm going to move home, back to my mother's, and go from there." She pauses. "We'll still be friends and see each other, right?"

"Of course. You are the only friend I have apart from Zuko and his brothers."

His brothers are finally growing to like me.

They seem more accepting, even if I am treated like a pest most of the time.

But I'm sure they love me. *Why wouldn't they?* Internally I laugh at my egotistical joke.

"You really don't know how amazing you are, Alaska. From the moment I met you, I knew you were special." She stands and goes to hug me, and I accept her hug and pat her back in an attempt to comfort her.

I know she needs this from me.

Even if I still hate affection.

The funny thing is—not from Zuko.

Zuko can hug me any day, and in any way, he pleases.

His affection I crave.

And I melt every single time.

In this series

Moments of Malevolence - (Zuko)
Moments of Madness - (Kyson)
Moments of Mayhem - (Kenzo)

Also by T.L Smith

Black (Black #1)

Red (Black #2)

White (Black #3)

Green (Black #4)

Kandiland

Pure Punishment (Standalone)

Antagonize Me (Standalone)

Degrade (Flawed #1)

Twisted (Flawed #2)

Distrust (Smirnov Bratva #1) FREE

Disbelief (Smirnov Bratva #2)

Defiance (Smirnov Bratva #3)

Dismissed (Smirnov Bratva #4)

Lovesick (Standalone)

Lotus (Standalone)

Savage Collision (A Savage Love Duet book 1)

Savage Reckoning (A Savage Love Duet book 2)

Buried in Lies

Distorted Love (Dark Intentions Duet 1)

Sinister Love (Dark Intentions Duet 2)

Cavalier (Crimson Elite #1)

Anguished (Crimson Elite #2)

Conceited (Crimson Elite #3)

Insolent (Crimson Elite #4)

Playette

Love Drunk

Hate Sober

Heartbreak Me (Duet #1)

Heartbreak You (Duet #2)

My Beautiful Poison

My Wicked Heart

My Cruel Lover

Chained Hands

Locked Hearts

Sinful Hands

Shackled Hearts

Reckless Hands

Arranged Hearts

Unlikely Queen

A Villain's Kiss

A Villain's Lies

Connect with T.L Smith by tlsmithauthor.com

About the Author

USA Today Best Selling Author T.L. Smith loves to write her characters with flaws so beautiful and dark you can't turn away. Her books have been translated into several languages. If you don't catch up with her in her home state of Queensland, Australia you can usually find her travelling the world, either sitting on a beach in Bali or exploring Alcatraz in San Francisco or walking the streets of New York.

Connect with me tlsmithauthor.com

Printed in Great Britain
by Amazon

25249432R00183